The Templarians

The Templarians

First published by Zoomwriters in 2023.
Printed in the UK.

Paperback edition:
ISBN: 9781914426742
Text copyright ©Creative Writing Club, 2023.
Cover design and layout: Lucy Meeber
Cover character art: Erin O'Neill
Edited by: Roya Mansour–Tehrani, James Turner, Daniella Sakota, Jessica, Lauren and Zillamog.

Layout by: LiteBook Prepress Services.
Cover copyright Creative Writing Club 2023.

THIS BOOK WAS CREATED AND WRITTEN BY:

Alex C, Damian, Ivan, Saxon, Freya, Harpreet and Leah.

Prologue

Teach me

The day was stormy and water was all around them. The New Templarian force was invading their home, the last thing they had. They broke down the door, smashed the equipment of the workshop and every last thing they owned.

There was a child in the building. His name will be known to you later. His mother was dead and his father was too important to be kept alive. His mother had been taken by the Templars and now his house was being taken. The forces had weapons, and the child's father was the target. The child had to hide in the secret tunnel, for his own safety, but his father wasn't quick enough. He heard a blaster shot ring throughout the building, as he ran, ran, and never looked back. He would make them pay, with or without their enemies.

"Father can't be dead," the child cried, now at the hidden base their father had set up.

"He...he didn't deserve to die," Alessandro said, "The Templarians will be after you,"

"Teach me then... magic."

"Gladly."

Chapter 1

Into the Fray

"My fellow Templarians," began the Grandmaster, "I have gathered you here because, although you might not be the best knights in our order, you deserve a chance to prove your courage."

The ancient leader of the Templarians paused for a moment, running his leathery fingers down his sword blade as the knights of the order listened to his every word. But one Templar was not listening.

His name was Nooble. This man had been unlucky ever since birth. He had no hair, it had all fallen out. Nooble was terrible at bets and gambling, after his first go, he had to quit the gambling business. All of his money flew away every time he opened his wallet. Nooble's only advantage was that he was pretty smart, even though no one took him seriously. That's why the Templarians wanted Nooble. He was the smartest one on the team.

Nooble didn't hear the rest of the Grandmaster's briefing. He'd practically passed out as soon as he realised that it was not a mistake – he really had been selected for an active combat mission. "Remind me what this is all about, Rorwa?" asked Nooble.

Rorwa sighed. She actually liked Nooble, but he could be extremely vexing at times. Why hadn't he been paying attention?

"A group of Templar scouts have disappeared in the far north, and it is suspected that the basilisk forces are to blame" explained Rorwa. "Our unit has been chosen to investigate. We leave in the morning," she ordered, walking out of the room in a rush to check on their supplies.

"What she just said," finished Vagar, meekly following her out.

As the unlikely group of heroes prepared to depart on their mission, not all of them were feeling confident about the journey ahead.

"I'm dead meat! They're going to kill me for sure!" Nooble was clumsy, but noble, smart, but often sick. Almost as if to prove it, Nooble had started to turn green. Mark, the Mage, ran up to him.

"Nooble! Why are you running away?" he cried.

"It's hopeless!" sighed Nooble. "I've been unlucky enough to fall into a pillow and get a feather in my eye, blinding me for 6 months! After that I fell down a well and lost my voice, meaning I stayed down there even longer. Then I fell in –"

"ALRIGHT! I don't need the details, Nooble!" interrupted Mark impatiently. Nooble groaned and walked away, but then, when he stepped on a stone, he stopped in his tracks. Funnily enough, nothing happened to him – it happened to Mark.

"AHHHHHHHHHH!" The wizard fell to the ground, screaming in fear – he had fallen in the well.

Nooble was surprised. Unlucky things happened to him, not anyone else. He was still nauseous however and promptly decided to vomit. *Maybe it was that stink in the well*, he thought.

In a moment of courage Nooble jumped down the hole to save Mark, but unsuccessfully. He squashed his yellow face against the stony floor. In the end it was up to Vagar to haul them out of the well so they could get on with leaving the Templar City.

Once they were all prepared, the group set off on their own to complete their mission. Rorwa chose to look after the unlucky Nooble for a while, since at lunch he had been walking with a bowl of soup when five dogs had come running down the steps. Nooble had fallen down a flight of stairs head first and hit himself extra hard, since he didn't have any hair to cushion the blow. The Templarians had been trying to find Nooble to use him for his smart mind. They hoped he would use his clever brain to become a good fighter. Rorwa knew that she didn't need any weapons to fight the basilisks that were injecting poison into innocent people. Instead of weapons, Rorwa had a unique power of her own that she had won many battles with: she could levitate objects.

Rorwa was practising her levitation skills when Nooble came up to her. "Rorwa, have you got any food, since I've just dropped my bowl because of your aerobatics?"

Seeing that Nooble was proving to be the weak link, Mark decided he would try and use his magic to give him some magical powers of his own, and get rid of his bad luck. He looked through his spell books that he had spent hours studying – Mark was a self–taught mage – until he found a suitable charm written in ancient runes. It would steal the luck from another creature and transfer it to Nooble. As he began to recite the spell the runes glowed green and came off the page, surrounding the Templarians. The runes swirled around Nooble, their lime green colour slowly seeping into him. Gradually, they slowed down and the colour drained out of them, leaving the symbols grey and falling apart. Nooble felt great, and, for the first time in his life, he felt lucky.

After a day of walking they stopped to rest and eat dinner. The group sat around a campfire and each took turns roasting the steak. Vagar and Rorwa, the two more experienced knights, had been arguing, and they decided to settle it in the forest circle, in a duel. Drawing swords, they began to fight. Nooble watched in awe as they fought, blades flying backwards and forwards. Rorwa lifted a tree trunk, crushed it and flung it towards Vagar, who was snarling like a wild werewolf. He had lost his sword, and was sweating profusely as he used his strange grey storm energy to deflect the shrapnel that Rorwa was shooting at him.

"Come then, great goddess," snarked Vagar, sarcasm dripping through his voice, as he used his grey storm powers to boost himself towards Rorwa. The effect only lasted long enough for him to smack into a large tree, flung at him by the residing master of gravity.

"Eat that, you little basil," she laughed victoriously as she pushed a pike–like tree branch closer and closer towards Vagar's throat.

The fight reminded her of the battle of Xangerit. Her mind flashed back as she pushed the weapon forward. In her mind, Rorwa was back there, an explosion behind her. Templarian and Hospitlar soldiers charged towards the enemy. Basilisk and mages responded, hurling fireballs and projectiles.

"Rorwa, follow me," shouted a young Vagar as he impaled a young mage.

"Come on," shouted Velostic, letting loose an arrow. Rorwa ran forward, getting trapped in the mud. The battle had been going on for several days and thousands of lives had been lost. The field that had once been solid ground had been reduced to mush.

"Cover me," called Vagar as he went to pull Rorwa up out of the ground, which was swallowing her up.

"Hurry up – we can't wait!" cried Velostic, ducking under a fireball.

Vagar pulled Rorwa out of the mud. "There, let's go!" But as the trio sprinted across the battlefield, they were surrounded by dark mercenaries and mages.

Remembering the times she and Vagar had fought alongside each other cooled Rorwa's temper, and the duel ended with the two shaking hands.

The next morning, after a night's rest at their camp, the group made their way into basilisk territory. Leaving the Templarian City and the forest far behind them, the terrain became rockier and the sky darkened overhead. Passing through an opening in the rocks, they found themselves winding their way through the snaky tunnels. As the knights walked further they began to hear the sounds of Templarian swords clashing with basilisk fangs. Vagar and Rorwa drew their weapons and prepared to fight. Nooble was frozen in fear, as the sounds grew nearer.

"Hey, Nooble!" Rorwa shouted.

"What?"

"I know that you've got your powers – Mark gave them to you. Now is the time to start using them!"

"Uh oh," said Nooble. "Maybe I am not that lucky after all."

But before Rorwa could even open her mouth in response, a huge basilisk crashed through the tunnel. Palious – the oldest and wisest of the Templarians – was under attack by one of the largest basilisks they had ever seen. Ripping, biting and killing – it was non–stop. Colossal razor–sharp teeth were digging into anything they could. Crimson, venomous blood gushed like a waterfall down the tunnel. Palious was experienced in fighting battles on his own in the past, but he had never seen any basilisks like this before.

Palious drew his sword, crusted with dried dragon blood from previous encounters. The basilisk dodged out of the way of the blade. Palious started to get impatient. He threw his sword in irritation, hoping that it would at least cut the monster on impact. But it failed. Vagar and Rorwa leapt in to try and fend off the beast, but the basilisk's snaking tail swept them up and pinned them to the wall. Mark focused all his energy into hexing the huge snake, but his magic was too weak to slow it. Nooble, even though he had new magic powers, stood shaking in his boots.

"What's wrong with you! Fight!" yelled Rorwa.

"This isn't the first time this has happened," Nooble whispered, under his breath. Nooble's borrowed powers were fading, right in the middle of a conflict with a deadly basilisk, more powerful than Nooble could reasonably fight.

As the green snake slithered across the cave mouth, the unit of Templarians guarding the tunnel raised the arms-cry. The basilisk's long fangs bit into the old Templarian warrior, and the iron armour did nothing to shield him. As swords clanged off the snake's long scales, the basilisk's eyes shifted from their yellow glow to a deep gold. Palious dropped limp from the serpent's mouth to the floor. Shockwaves spread through the Templarian soldiers as they realised that their wise old commander was dead.

A gust of wind blew around the cave and sand suddenly filled the air of the tunnel.

"Where did that sandstorm come from? Argh!" A soldier fell victim to the sand biting his eyes. The basilisk, visibly unperturbed, continued shredding the Templarian force and the acting commander ordered a retreat.

After the defeat, the Templarians regrouped outside the tunnels, hanging their heads in shame that they didn't do more to save Palious. They were especially disappointed in Nooble, and knew he would have to be punished if the Templarian leaders found out. Nooble himself was oblivious.

Unsuccessful, the unit made the journey back to the city.

Chapter 2

Nooble's Punishment

Back at the Templarian City, the friends still felt betrayed by their companion, and decided to confront him.

"Nooble, we need to speak to you," called Rorwa, her arm in a sling.

Vagar followed, sporting a blood stained bandage wrapped around his chest. They walked side by side, looking as murderous as a dying dog.

"My apologies, but I have a study class on broken bones," lied Nooble.

"Nooble, I could gut you," said Vagar, gripping his sword to emphasise his point.

"You think threatening to gut him will help?" Rorwa tipped an ice-cold bucket of water over Nooble's feet.

"Well, I'll be going," whispered Nooble, sheepishly inching out of the corner he was trapped in.

"No; you will be staying here for a long time, while you explain why you didn't use your new powers to kill that basilisk," snarled Vagar.

As they argued, the Head of Templarian Magic passed them, and ensured they knew they had been overheard. "I heard that," snapped the Head. The group turned around in shock.

Nooble fell to his knees and begged. He knew that people who didn't fight hard enough would be sent away to a work camp, or to an underground prison, only fed rotten sprouts every day... Or worse...

"Oh, please don't send me away!" he moaned. "Spare my life, *please!*"

"Very well! You will live, but you will be put on trial for cowardice" sighed the Head. "Rorwa, Vagar, chain him up!"

Vagar was ready to pounce on the chains and wrap him up in seconds, but Rorwa was reluctant. "Can we just let him go, Sir?" she asked.

Vagar leapt in. "Just tie him up! The sooner we're done, the sooner we go for lunch!"

"Is that all you care about?" Rorwa said, shocked that Vagar would choose lunch over Nooble.

Rorwa and Vagar argued and argued. The Head sighed. He was used to this.

Rorwa and Vagar eventually did as they were told, and thirty minutes and a lot of broken chains later, they were finished. But the chains fell off again.

"Can't I just walk?" Nooble said impatiently.

When they arrived at Nooble's Hearing, the citizens were waiting curiously to uncover Nooble's reason for failing to fight. Nooble was taken before the Head, who acted as the Judge.

"I am Vordrag, the Head of Magic and the Judge of this Order. Now, Nooble," said Vordrag, "how do you explain yourself?"

Nooble fidgeted nervously. "So…" He struggled to get the words out until he blurted: "my powers don't work properly; I haven't had enough training; I can't kill my enemies without hurting myself, and Vagar keeps criticising me." Nooble stopped and looked at Vagar, who had started to sweat. Nooble had hoped Vagar would get into trouble. How wrong he was.

"Your explanation is not good enough!" yelled Vordrag fiercely. Everyone outside on the streets stopped and stared at them both.

Nooble was upset with himself for getting into this. "Please, I won't do it again, please, I promise!" he begged helplessly.

Vordrag was a short, shrivelled man who had a nose like a pointed hat. He was known to be powerful. Although he was a dwarfish looking sneak everybody still respected him. Vordrag had ears like dead petals. His skin looked like something had sucked all of the moisture out of him and left him withered.

"I've had enough of your nonsense!" he bellowed.

Nooble pleaded, but Vordrag only roared in response, "You will be sent to a work camp, where you will be breaking rocks everyday!"

As he broke the granite rock at the camp, Nooble thought: *was the luck not working*? Why was he being blamed for not turning enemies into cacti? He was trying his best to fight, but he just wasn't good at that sort of thing. The granite wasn't giving way, and the brick he was supposed to be chiseling fell apart. His muscles were burning, and night was a long way off.

He looked in disgust at the bowl of carrots the workers had been given.

"Eat it," grunted the Cook. "It's the only food you'll get."

"B– b– b– but I don't like carrots" replied Nooble, trying to appear as innocent as possible.

Before he knew it, he was eating mashed carrot with roast carrot steak with carrot chips for a snack. Only one person ate it with a happy expression on his face.

"Who are you?" asked Nooble, curious as to who this strange carrot connoisseur might be.

"I am the carrot god's greatest follower, bane of those who don't eat carrots, the wielder of the golden carrot and the one who has visited every carrot god altar and sacrificed carrots. If you don't like carrots I will sacrifice you to the carrot god." Nooble just looked at him in confusion and apprehension. "Oh, tomorrow I have scheduled a sacrifice to the celery god," the carrot man continued.

"Don't listen to him – he's mad. He worships a new god every day," said the Cook.

Nooble knew he was going to be stuck in the torturous prison for a long time and he wasn't sure how much longer he could last. It was midday and they had stopped breaking rocks. In the huge hall at the centre of the prison camp everyone was lined up in a snaking queue, waiting to get their soggy cabbage.

"Next!" ordered the Cook.

A prisoner complained. "This is horrible food!"

"Be quiet and eat! One more complaint and there will be no supper for you," yelled the Cook in response.

Nooble had been in the camp for five months, but his sentence was ten years. When he overheard that the punishments were about to get harsher, Nooble decided that he had no choice – he had to break out. But to do that, he needed help.

He tried to talk to two fellow inmates near his ward. "Hello, can I talk to –"

"Push off, Noob!" growled the tall, skinny prisoner.

"Stop shouting, please" begged the big, burly prisoner.

These two seemed to have their roles swapped.

"You're talking about an escape plan, right?" said Nooble.

The skinny prisoner narrowed his eyes. "Yeah… maybe."

"Well, the truth is," started the burly prisoner, "we successfully escaped the prison, but not the guards."

"Shut up, James!" the thin prisoner barked.

"Okay, Arcus, but I'm not a liar!"

Arcus glared at James. "Why did you give away my name?"

"Hey, you three!" said a guard. "Nooble, come here! What are you lot plotting?"

"How come your face looks even more ugly behind a mask?" Nooble quipped. James gave him a little sign for him to stop; Arcus put his head in his hands.

Later that day, Nooble was sitting at the table eating his dinner with bruises on his face. Arcus came and sat next to him. "Want some food?" James sat down next to Arcus, but then the carrot man came and sat down as well.

"You should believe in yourself!" the carrot man said. "Believe in your bruises."

James and Nooble looked at him like he was crazy. Because he was.

"How does carrot man get all these gods?" asked Nooble.

"Wellmfyoumfshouldseemfhiscellwallmf," said James, his mouth full of food. Once he'd finished chewing, he added, "He has a name, by the way. Michael. Not 'carrot man'. Michael."

So the boys took James' suggestion and went to see Michael's cell wall.

"Huh!" Nooble touched the wall lightly. "So he keeps track of days by gods?" Instead of tallying the days on the wall as time passed, Michael appeared to have wedged in vegetables, and other random objects. It was like a mosaic dedicated to his lunacy.

"I think he's been here for three years," said Arcus. "There's a good amount of cucumbers! Carrots! Celery! Ketchup! Corners! Walls! Cells! The walls, not the skin cells."

Nooble tripped over a board sticking out. "Argh!" Arcus gave his friend a hand. "I think I figured it out!" said Nooble.

"Figured out what?"

Nooble looked at the board under his feet. "How to escape. But," he said as he looked up at the cell walls, "we're going to need Michael the carrot man's help…"

"I hate this plan!" bawled Michael, holding a potato. The group were climbing across Michael's cell wall to reach a hole in the roof. They were almost at the top, about to escape through a gap.

"Shut up!" hissed Nooble, suddenly seeing the potato in Michael's hands, "Why did you bring that?" he said panicking – but it was too late. The potato floated up into the air and glowed red. The potatoes in the prison were especially made to detect potential escapees, and if potatoes were carried outside the cells and dining rooms they glowed to give an emergency signal.

It wasn't long before Nooble was sitting miserably again in his ice–cold cell. Their escape attempt had failed. They would spend the rest of their lives here working as slave labourers. He longed for his friends' warm presence. He sat motionless on the wet stones, too tired, drained and angry to cry.

The cell door opened and three prisoners were shoved in. The rusting, iron bar door was closed with a clang. Nooble didn't feel like visitors.

"Hello," he muttered without looking up, "I'm a dead man named Nooble."

"Well, Mr. Dead Man," said the voice of the new prisoner, "we are here for an alive man named Nooble." Nooble looked up; it was Vagar. Vagar laid his hand on his silver spear with lightning bolts engraved upon it, as if to make a move towards him, but suddenly it seemed as if he was grabbing Nooble from behind his neck. His face was an inch from Nooble's, as he embraced him in an awkward hug.

"Let's get out of here, you little basilisk tooth! Or I will do something that will haunt your nightmares," spat a woman from behind him, viciously pulling a knife from her hair. Rorwa clearly wasn't enthusiastic about being in the cell.

"Orgiua Fristin Rorwa! What's wrong? Are you oka–" Vagar began, before a hand was clasped across his mouth.

"If you say what I think you are about to say, then I might kill you. I hate being pitied," warned Rorwa. "We're happy to see you, Nooble," she added.

"Well, your expression of happiness is lovely, but we have a job to do," said the third prisoner.

"Shut up Mark," barked Vagar and Rorwa at the same time. The unassuming figure stepped quietly out of the shadows.

"Mark!" gasped Nooble. "What are you doing here?"

Chapter 3

The Great Escape

Nooble was incredulous that his old friends – as far as they might be called friends – were here, in his cell, and they seemed to want to break him out.

"*Psst!*" hissed another voice.

Vagar looked over towards another cell.

"Who are these two?" asked Vagar.

"The skinny one is called Arcus, and the fat man is James," Nooble answered.

"Did he call me fat?" moaned James. "That is so mean!"

"We're here to bust you out!" Rorwa whispered to Nooble.

"Legally?"

"Of course not!" said Mark. But, before they could do anything, three tall guards burst into the cell.

"What is going on, you ungrateful wretches?" the first one bellowed. They had overheard the plotting and became suspicious.

"Nothing, nothing!" Rorwa said, unconvincingly. The guards ran towards them to tie them up, but Mark conjured a spell and blasted the three guards. Another spell broke down the cell doors; James, Arcus, Michael, Nooble, Rorwa and Vagar crashed out of their cells.

But the floorboards underneath them were old and rickety, and with the weight of all eight of them crashing onto it, the boards fell apart, and the gang found themselves lying on the icy ground underneath the prison. Mark saw a light.

"Follow me!" he cried. The others followed and they opened an ice door. It was a snowy plain.

"Let's go," said Rorwa. She walked through the snow and the others followed, except for James and Arcus. They left the others, and ran in a different direction. Nooble wanted to go back for them, but Mark said to forget them.

The remaining few trudged on. Soon enough, the gang could

feel the cold seeping into their bones. Nooble's prisoner attire was hardly warm enough for the prison itself, let alone the icy tundra they found themselves in now. They were freezing, and in severe danger of frostbite and hypothermia. Mark looked at his friends, shivering and afraid of what the cold night would bring. Mark couldn't let it be death. He needed to cast a spell to keep them warm, and quickly. Closing his eyes, he focused for a minute. He let the power of his magic flood his veins and every facet of his being, and cast a new spell – one that would protect them all from the freezing ice and snow. They felt warmth flooding into them.

"Can I have some more of that luck thing Mark?"

"No," said Mark. His voice was calm but he was visibly exhausted from using his magic so much. "It takes a lot of energy, and I don't have endless amounts. There's still a very unlucky rabbit bouncing around from the last time."

"Oh, well," replied Nooble, but he obviously didn't care much about the rabbit.

Back at the prison, the guards were in a state of emergency. "All of you! Find those prisoners before midnight or there'll be no meals for a month!" yelled Yshkavis. She had always been a fierce person. After she took over control of the prison, both prisoners and wardens alike had grown to fear the iron–willed Etherian and her motto didn't make the situation any lighter – "*There is No Comedy in a Prison.*"

Yshkavis was the daughter of the prison's founder, Sir Exevra, who had died when she was 17. Yshkavis always hated it when people bullied her for her strange name in school, and even most of the teachers couldn't pronounce it. She and her few friends were the only people who would pronounce it 'yoush–kra–vich', as it was originally intended to be pronounced. This cruelty in her childhood heavily reflects in her current behaviour – when she became head, no-one respected her. Yshkavis had had to earn her position, as no-one would respect a female, let alone an Etherian. In retrospect, those workers would regret that. She had no mercy, or so people thought…

Yshkavis was not pleased at the news, summoning the guards to the titanium-lined meeting room. "We have a black alert. Prisoners from cell B-264 have reached the outer borders of cell-block B. They shall be found immediately and brought to me, or you will face Ikari's wrath," she commanded from her office. Ikari growled at the camera to show the workers their place.

"One of you useless drones must have seen something!" Mr. Job barked from her side, and Yshkavis ordered a Class X lock down and a full search of every cell. This was the first time Yshkavis had had to deal with an escape, but with her knowledge of the prison, sword–fighting, and the assistance of her pet Ikari, there was no possible chance of escape, Mr. Job thought. Little did they know who they were up against…

Every single guard knew that they had to find the escapees or they would face serious consequences. Yshkavis could count on only one man – her weathered sidekick – Mr. Job.

Mr. Bob Job (yes, that was his first name) was always being yelled at by his mother. Most of the time he was said to be plain stupid – which was sort of true. But no prisoner would ever dare to say that to his face. Mr. Job had turned his depression into anger. Then he was posted to the ice prison on Earth 2. It was located on a remote snowy plain somewhere in the valleys of Snowyplainia. His boss, Yshkavis was always yelling at him. But he couldn't resign. If he did, he would be shot. But that went for everyone in the prison. Sometimes, you couldn't leave the prison job even though you were old. Usually, the guards would get shot by their superiors. Mr. Job, the guards, the officers and the prisoners were all miserable. The only person who was happier was Yshkavis, living in luxury all the time. But Mr. Job never got money.

Yshkavis would *say* he would get more than one hundred thousand gold coins.

But he never got anything. Just a mouldy old piece of cheese. Yes, he was truly a miserable person.

"HAVE YOU FOUND THE PRISONERS YET?!" bellowed Yshkavis.

"Uhhhhhhhhhhhhhhhh–" uuuhhhed Mr. Job before being interrupted again.

"IF YOU DON'T REPORT BACK TO ME IN FIVE SECONDS, I WILL NOT GIVE YOU YOUR PAYCHECK!"

"What paycheck?" asked Mr. Job.

"THAT PAYCHECK!" yelled Yshkavis. She pointed at a blank space on the wall.

"Are you going to give me your office?" asked Mr. Job in delight. His eyes looked like stars.

"What? NO! YOU'RE JUST A SERVANT! YOU'RE FIRED!" Yshkavis and pointed to the door.

Mr. Job exclaimed in delight and ran out of the door, but he didn't hear what she had to say next:

"Guards, have him shot."

She went out to check, only to see a very strange sight. All the prisoners were snoring and the guards and officers had... disappeared?

Bellowing in anger, Yshkavis reached down and tried to pull out a pistol, but she couldn't find it. "Where did that gun go?" she asked herself.

Luckily for Mr. Job, her pistol had fallen and broken behind her.

The guards from the prison cells had gone on a hunt to track down the groups of prisoners. Joining the guards were wolf–like creatures that breathed fire. Called Lykos, they are known to be aggressive and beastly. These lupine beasts had the speed of a hundred cheetahs combined, so the guards had not been able to keep up with the Lykos.

Yshkavis and her talking Lyko, Ikari, had been living on the planet Didos – all of the people of this sand planet had their own Lyko, but Ikari was extraordinary. The gigantic lupine beast had several rows of razor–sharp teeth to protect its owner and attack its enemy. Lykos were known for defending their owner to the death. He was the leader of the Lykos and he had the unique attribute of near immortality.

"Go and find the prisoners before midnight or you'll be sleeping outside in the snow!" Yshkavis ordered.

There was no news on the missing prisoners, which angered and frustrated her to no end. Her last hope was Ikari; he had run at lightning speed past the guards and out of the well–protected gates, on the hunt, intent on not coming back until he dragged with him the prisoners.

Nooble trudged on behind Vagar, who had a disgruntled Rorwa on his shoulders as she had hurt her leg by slipping in front of a falling rock. They had to walk on icy mountain paths, and with both of them slower than usual, they were easy targets for falling stones.

"Come on, we're nearly there," said Nooble.

"We have to jump over the entrance gate. It's metres high," grumbled Vagar. "Why did you have to hurt yourself? I'll have to lift you!" His shoulder was starting to hurt. Rorwa was smaller than him, but she seemed as heavy as two bulls.

"Stop complaining!" growled Rorwa, wincing in pain.

"Nooble first, then Michael, then me, and then finally Vagar and Rorwa," ordered Mark, frustrated with Vagar and Rorwa's constant arguing.

Nooble jumped the gate. Michael, insisting the cat goddess Miawa would help him, jumped the gate too. He proceeded to thank Miawa over and over again. Mark levitated over – his magic had grown stronger. Now it was Vagar's turn. Even though he had storm powers, the prison had halted them, and he was weakened by carrying Rorwa on the journey.

He jumped. Time slowed down as he leapt; but he was nowhere near.

Suddenly gunfire erupted at his back, sending them crashing to the ground. Rorwa didn't fare much better, crashing down to cold rocky ground. By the time they'd both come to, a thousand guards seemed to have appeared out of every inch of the complex, homing in on the two fallen knights. They were armed to the teeth with guns, crossbows, spears and anything else they'd confiscated from the prisoners.

Rorwa levitated a large stone between her and the incoming forces. She turned around to face the rest of the group.

"Run like a river – the great hunter is on your heels!" Rorwa cried, trying to wake the wolfish man that was Vagar.

"But what about you and Vagar?" Nooble's eyes were like a conflicted child, staring across the gate that separated them.

"We are survivors of many things – war and battle are just another one of them."

Mark thought that she reminded him of a goddess, a specific one. What was her name? Minerva, that was it. Goddess of war and wisdom. She seemed too wise to look so young.

"Come. They will do what must be done for the rest of us to escape," a grim look on his shadowed features. He nodded to Rorwa, knowing she would likely die a death worthy of the greatest warrior.

Rorwa knew it was her elected duty to fight and die, if that was what had to be done. She could not imagine the idea of failing in battle.

Meanwhile, the Lykos were travelling up the steep, never-ending mountains on the hunt for the escaped prisoners, running up and down the icy hills. In the distance, some prisoners had been seen running across a field of stunted vegetables. One silhouette was tall and skinny, the other one was round and burly. A stampede of frozen feet had rushed past the gates and through to the field.

"Catch them!"

Left lying on the icy ground, Rorwa (as usual) was most alert to the approach of the guards. First she heard the deep barking of the Lykos; narrowing her eyes, the sight of dozens of guards rushing after them only confirmed what she already knew. Panic and adrenaline coursing through her, Rorwa kicked Vagar not so gently with her good leg. She hovered over the cold, rocky ground. Her chest hurt. But she soldiered on; if they were captured alive, they would have the devil to pay.

"Stop hitting me, you evil beast," Vagar snarled, suddenly awake. He got to his feet, his shirt ripped in the back from the blast, and Rorwa pushed him around to see the prison guards coming their way.

"Well, if this is our last time on this earth, I'm glad to go down fighting. It was an honour serving with you." He lit his hands with electricity.

"I'm with you there," nodded Rorwa, preparing to fight to her last.

Then all hell broke loose.

Rock fragments flew; a small army of guards charged forward. Arrows flew over their heads, and Vagar leapt into the sky, electricity flowing up and down his arms. As he positioned himself in the air, a small tornado surrounded him. When he landed, he brought with him a huge explosion, throwing back almost all the closest guards.

Vagar punched a soldier in the ribs, hearing a sickening crack. Lightning surrounded him as he grabbed another by the throat and shot a thousand bolts into his body, killing him instantly. Then with all his strength, he kicked another in the chest, sending him flying pathetically, like a rag doll.

Covered from arrow fire by Rorwa, he summoned a huge

electric storm around him; all that was left afterwards of the enemies were a few charred remains, and Vagar himself.

Then a gurgled cry diverted his attention. Rorwa, who had been covering Vagar from the mountain above the complex, and deflecting arrows, had been struck by what looked like a javelin to the shoulder.

Vagar's lapse in focus had let the guards gain an advantage, as he tried to reach his mortally wounded friend.

A barbed arrow struck his stomach.

Then another.

Guards scrambled towards them like starved beasts; Rorwa and Vagar were just meat to them.

Chains wrapped around his neck, arms and legs. He strained against them desperately, trying to run, but he was only one person.

They forced him to the ground, and soon everything went black.

In her metallic office, the feared Yshkavis was cleaning, when the door was opened by her assistant, Mr Job. As she had predicted, he had come crawling back to beg for his job – it was the only thing he knew how to do. The iron-plated door opened with a near silent whoosh, and the blue lights that came on made a barely noticeable hum.

"Miss, we have a report on the escapees," Mr Job said, in his scratchy voice.

"Call me Ma'am, or I won't miss my shot. I am tired of the disrespect I get on a daily basis. Don't add to that, Mr Job," Yshkavis responded harshly. She put her coffee down on a black place mat, on her dark grey desk, as Ikari growled.

"Sorry, Ma'am," Mr Job said, petrified. "We have captured two of the escapees, but the others have seemingly disappeared."

Yshkavis' face tightened.

"I suppose I'll have to do this myself," she said. "Haven't got my hands dirty in a while..."

Chapter 4

A Charged Encounter

Vagar woke up in a dark room. It smelled of blood. The enclosed walls echoed the screams of the others unfortunate enough to be there.

The Tower of the Bone-Breakers was a place that only officials of the highest rank knew about. Vagar looked around, only just noticing the fact he was chained to the floor, and something cold was touching his side. He turned his head to the side to see Rorwa just as harshly chained next to him.

"Commanders." Vagar looked up at the new voice. "I welcome you to my tower."

If he didn't have whiplash already, he definitely did now.

"I have to say," the voice said, "I was rather surprised when two of the greatest field commanders of the Order in recent history were being sent to my tower to be broken for treason."

It was jailor Vorani Vordik. Vagar would have strangled the basilisk hatchling, if only he could get his hands on him.

"Get out of here," hissed Vagar, using all his strength to strain against the chains, cutting his wrists in the process.

"Silence," snarled Vordik as he pulled out a metal barbed whip. He struck Vagar on the back for the insolence he had shown, but then he hit Rorwa, too. The sudden pain woke her up very efficiently. Her once silky hair was matted and coated in mud, and her face covered in nasty black bruises.

"You son of a–" exclaimed Rorwa, but she was slapped before she could finish.

"You don't speak unless spoken to." Vagar managed to knee him in the ribs, but Vordik simply straightened himself before striking Vagar clean across his face.

"Now I ask you – why did you break the failure Nooble out of the work camp?" asked Vordik.

"We will never answer your questions, you little turnip!" cried Rorwa, as she was whipped for her bravery.

"I will ask you again tomorrow. If you don't answer by then, I will bring out the burning rods."

They cursed under their breath as he left the cell with a clang, and a promise of fresh torture when the sun rose. They both asked the same question without making a noise: *Do we tell him?*

The sunrise came and with it arrived Vordik's torture. "I will ask you once again: how and why did you break Nooble out?"

"Burn in the fires of Vortias, you mule!" spat Rorwa.

Vordik didn't respond. Instead, he walked out of the cell, returning with a burning rod, glowing red with the heat of a thousand suns. Rorwa's screams would haunt Vagar for the rest of his life.

But soon it was his turn. The rod pressed into his lower neck, right on the spine. It was like nothing he had ever felt. He could hear a scream that didn't seem like his own, when the rod was finally removed. Sadistically, Vordik smiled. "You'll be left for a week with no food and daily questioning. I suggest you start opening up."

The week went slowly for the duo. With daily whippings and no food, life was living hell. But they had to survive, they had to protect Nooble. It would go against Templarian code to betray him and reveal their mission.

On one particularly harsh day, Vordik laughed as he looked at a tray of torture weapons. He pondered for a second, then picked up a sword handle. "You will like this one," he muttered. "This device is an electrical generator and conductor. It conducts electricity towards a general area. Field Commander Vagar, you will be its first test subject."

This could be it. This could be their chance. How stupid was Vordik, to try to punish a Storm Power with electricity? This is what Vagar was built for. He felt the lightning hit, but it only singed his chest. He controlled the lightning, letting it surround him. He used it to burn through the chains holding him up, and soon dropped to the floor.

Vordik was too distracted by torturing Rorwa to realise that Vagar had escaped until his rough hand gripped around Vordik's throat. He looked into his eyes, giving Vordik a taste of his own medicine: an electric shock that killed him instantly.

"Are you alright?" he asked, his lips raw from lack of water.

"Magnificent," said Rorwa sarcastically. Vagar let out a dry laugh.

"Come on, let's get out of here," said Vagar.

Adrenaline was the only thing keeping them working, but it was a finite resource, and they had very little time to escape before the guards realised something was wrong. Running through the prison, they finally saw the exit, but it was guarded by at least ten guards. "I'll deal with the guys on the left, you take the right," Vagar whispered to Rorwa, as he prepared for an ambush.

When he leapt from cover, he punched one man in the neck and kicked another in the stomach. He saw Rorwa somehow using five swords to duel three guards. Talented girl. Summoning lightning, he disintegrated two more guards, only to have a crossbow bolt embed itself in his upper thigh courtesy of the fifth guard. Grunting in pain, he sent a jolt of electricity running down his feet, and finished him off in revenge.

The only way to go was up. Literally. Their only option was to levitate and fly away, but it took so much energy and they were both exhausted. But Vagar picked Rorwa up, and focused on trying to get afloat in the air. Rorwa had never flown before; she had levitated off the ground, but nothing like this. Vagar was known to be one of the best fliers in the Commanders.

"It's magical," breathed Rorwa. "Do you do this often?" She waited for a response but all she got was the whistling sound of the mountains passing by them.

"Vagar? Vagar, hello, Earth to Vagar," she said, smacking him between the shoulders. Still nothing; then she realised they were quickly declining. He had lost consciousness! "For the love of all things holy!" she screamed, before passing out along with Vagar.

Tumbling through the tundra, with the wind whipping their clothes and unconscious faces, the two plummeted to the earth. It was a miracle they landed in a patch of soft snow that had only fallen recently. The impact jolted them both conscious again. Pain blurred Vagar's sight as his side throbbed from the fall and harsh contact.

Rubbing the snow from his face and his back, Vagar tried to stand up and take in his surroundings. "Where are we?" Rorwa whispered to him in a low voice.

The unforgiving wind was gusting all around them both. "I

don't know – it's too cold… Rorwa, I can't focus. I need to rest!"

Vagar nearly hadn't noticed the small but poisonous snake slithering on the rock he was about to step on. Exclaiming, he drew back his foot, ready to crush the serpent with the sole of his thick leather boot, but Rorwa put a restraining hand on his shoulder.

"Let it live!" she said.

By now several Lamian officers, snake–like, Basilisk underlings, were in the area, and hundreds of serpent infantry were surrounding them. Vagar was once again chained up – not with chains this time, but with snakes. So, snaked up.

"The heir is here, the heir has arrived," a Lamian said excitedly. Or maybe we should say: a Lamian officer hissed. Its long teeth and thin forked tongue made it difficult to understand its words, but its murderous expression was not difficult to understand at all.

"I swear, I should've hunted these filthy creatures to extinction," roared Vagar, as he ripped the snakes off him and leapt up in anger.

Several snakes launched themselves at him, but his body was like an electric conductor, and he fried the creatures like eggs on a pan. He grasped a snake around its ice cold, slimy body, and squeezed with all his strength. He heard the crunching of bones and didn't bother to look. Then, out of nowhere, there came an acidic spray of venom from the little snake struggling in his hand, blasting him right in his shoulder.

"It burns!" he howled.

A strong hiss dragged his attention away. He looked at the Lamian snake to the left of him, but its lips were still, and the hiss was too loud for a smaller snake to have made.

He looked at Rorwa – only to be shocked by what he saw.

She was making the sound.

Her mouth was wide open, hissing with hideously loud intensity; her tongue seemed to stretch painfully out beyond where it should. He couldn't make out the look in her eyes or what on earth she was doing, but all he knew was that it was helping: he looked at the snakes surrounding them, and all of them were bowed in submission before her.

Then they began slithering into formation around her.

"What in the name of death itself have you done?" he

exclaimed, charging up to Rorwa.

He felt betrayed. He had grown up with Rorwa almost from birth, what was she doing talking to their enemy snakes? The basilisks? And why could they understand her?

"Stop!" she roared, her voice silencing the area. The snakes surrounded her, like a bodyguard. "What have you done, Rorwa?" she heard Vagar rage, charging up to the snakes surrounding her. They hissed at him threateningly, as if to protect her.

"I don't know," she said, exasperatedly raising her hands. "I really don't know."

Chapter 5

The Crystal Caverns

At that very moment, far beneath them, a serpent was slithering through The Crystal Caverns, the home of the basilisks, where he had lived his entire life. The massive crystal formations, with their glittering purple light, out sized him, and beneath them he felt very, very small.

Around the corner was the snack bar, and beside that stood the science lab. The science lab was off limits. It could only be entered if you had had special training on particular machines. Zaps and crashes could be heard from outside the locked metal room. All sorts of machines could be seen from the glass windows. Recently, due to the war, the scientists had been working on unique heated armour for the army of basilisks. Any basilisk who dared to enter the lab would be severely punished.

Behind the snack bar was a door that led to the food processing centre. It was the place where annoying humans were killed and served up, but not before they had been checked for poison. It was very gruesome. Their hair was like chocolate to the basilisks who ate every bit of human meat. Only the Food–Processor Lamians knew about what the basilisks ate. The cold drinks were snake–milk, water, and fizzy drinks like Coca–Snake, Shredding–Hawk, and Lepsi (which was named after the Lamians). They always checked the wine and barrels of beer before they were sold to the public. They took practically everything out and replaced it with food colouring and warm water. Some basilisks complained about it when they first had it, but they were sent to solitary confinement. So no one bought the wine and beer. At least they didn't drink alcohol. It's bad for you.

The head of the food processing centre was called Arda. He used to run a shop called Asda, but someone closed him down due to a copyright issue. So he opened up a shop called Aldi, but then someone else closed him down. So he took his spaceship and went down to planet Earth, arrived where the two supermarket chains were, and went briefly to give the owner a slap and gave the other owner a slap, before going back to the Basilisk Planet. But his fuel ran out, so he got stuck in space for three Basilisk months (three human years), and when he was finally rescued he was taken to the wrong place on the planet, then got involved in the Great Basilisk War, and finally came home to the Crystal Caverns, where he got a job as the Head of the Food Processing Centre in Baskovy City.

The Head of the Food Processing Centre sounds grand, doesn't it? Well, it was, because it was the highest and only rank in the company. In fact, he was the only person working there.

That's why he was always grumpy and sad. Every time he saw someone, he would growl. The only thing he liked was sleeping, which he got thirty Basilisk minutes (or three human hours) of a day. He had had enough of working alone at the Food Processing Centre. He thought it was about time for a change.

Elsewhere in the caverns there was a huge commotion, as the Lamians heard rumours that some Templarians had broken in. They scrambled to collect weapons from the wooden racks. Among them was Lmia, a high ranking Lamian warrior, who grabbed a scimitar with her scaly hand. This particular weapon was important to basilisk culture, because they were awarded to Captain Lamians, just one rank before becoming a full-blown Basilisk. Lmia was a fierce warrior.

Just then, the invaders burst through the Crystal Gates. Two Templarians stumbled in, fighting off the Lamians who had pursued them through the tundra and down through the tunnels. Though the Lamians had gravitated towards Rorwa, they would not side with the Templarians against their fellow snakes. Lmia looked over at the one who the Councilor had charged her with. She recognised him. Named Vagar, she knew he was of northern origin. She hissed with displeasure; he was taller than her by two fangs.

Vagar glared at the snakes, his face stony like a cliff against an ocean wave. He shoved his way through the horde, earning irritated hisses. He grabbed a half sword from the rack, not realising the disrespect he was committing to basilisk culture – the weapon could be held by generals only.

"Put the sacred blade back, invader," hissed Lmia, rising to her full height.

"Make me," Vagar said, bowing with fake respect and a sickly smile drawn across his features. Lmia launched herself at Vagar, her weapon aimed at his heart. She would get in trouble for attacking him like this – the Councilor wanted them alive – but it would not be enough to stain her record. A smirk appeared on her dark olive green skin.

The glaive blade inched closer to Vagar's heart. The steel caught the light. Vagar stood to one side. Time seemed to slow down as Vagar impaled the Lamian soldier in the stomach. Warm blood spilled down Vagar's hand in rivulets, making its way to drip onto the floor. He kicked the body off his blade. His bare feet gripped the warm sand that covered the floor of the cavern. He raised the blade in a defensive stance, and impaled her again.

"I will kill you," she roared, using her powerful tail to launch herself towards Vagar.

As they locked blades she was pushed back. Amazingly, the human overpowered her, making her slither away and grab another scimitar. She was hurt now, but Lmia grew stronger the angrier she got. She coiled her tail and leapt at Vagar again. This time he was caught off guard, and the Lamian Captain knocked him to the floor. She had her glaive pointed against the Templarian's throat. Her smile appeared again.

Just then Rorwa jumped into her and drove her own half-sword through the Lamian Captain's heart. She reached down and hauled Vagar to his feet. They looked around, and found themselves faced with a hundred blades. Even they couldn't escape from this one.

'Capture them!" called the biggest of the serpents. "Take them prisoner!" Rorwa and Vagar looked at each other, then let the guards tie them up. They were marched down the tunnel by laughing Lamians, who couldn't help but think how tasty they'd be.

Elsewhere in the Crystal Caverns, Emperor Sxxx the 223st slithered through the royal quarters that were carved by his predecessor, Emperor Sxxx the 1st. Unfortunately, and confusingly, all emperors had to be called Sxxx. It was a shame. Emperor Sxxx the 223st would have preferred the name John.

Emperor Sxxx had always been fascinated by the Templarians

and their exotic names. Blooble, Jemba, Bob – somehow they had a pleasant sound that basilisk names never had. He had always wanted to be called John. John seemed to suit him.

The snake king had it hard. He had to call himself Sxxx when he was in an official meeting, or when talking to his followers, but in his mind he was always John. If he ever got confused, at the wrong moment, this would lead to scandals.

For example, once he declared, "I, Emperor John the 223st, hereby allow you to mine crystals in the new territory that you discovered!"

This led to his advisor whispering into his ear urgently, "Sir, your name is Sxxx, not John, where did you even get the John from?"

"Oh yeah, sorry. I, Emperor Sxxx the 223st allow you to mine crystals in the new place you discovered."

The burrowers who had been waiting for these words replied, "As you wish Emperor, so it shall be!" and quickly left to mine crystals.

He had got away with it then, but worried that his followers were getting suspicious. He worried a lot. It was very stressful being an emperor.

Chapter 6

Old Friends, New Troubles

Far away from the royal quarters, Vagar and Rorwa were waking up slowly. They had been knocked out and couldn't remember anything after the battle. Vagar looked up drowsily at the stone walls.

"We're in a prison, again!?" screamed Vagar. "WHHYYY!?"

"Because we are," sighed Rorwa. All of Vagar's screaming had woken Mark.

"Shut up!" he sighed. He threw his pillow at Vagar, who threw it back. Then Mark whacked Vagar with it, and Vagar did it back. Soon they were smothering each other and screaming like fighting children. Which they were. Rorwa sighed.

Then, suddenly, she realised something. She grabbed Vagar off Mark and chucked him against the wall. "Ow!" he said, rubbing his head. "That hurt'"

"Mark, what are you doing here?" she asked the mage. "I thought you had escaped with Nooble and the others."

"I did," Mark said, glaring at Vagar. "But I saw that you'd got caught and thought you could use some help. I used a spell to get through the gates, but not long after that the basilisks caught me. Now I'm wishing I hadn't bothered." He glared at Vagar. "Nooble's gone on to Templarian City, to tell them that you've been captured by the basilisks."

"That wasn't very clever, they'll throw him back in prison!" Rorwa moaned.

"Very helpful of you to get caught straight away," said Vagar, smirking.

"You got caught as well, meat–head!" said the mage. Rorwa groaned. She'd had enough of them already.

She walked over to the door of the cell and looked out. She looked at the two idiots. Then she looked down and saw something horrible in the corner! "AUUUGGHHHH!!!" screamed Rorwa, jumping up. She inspected it.

There was something seeping out of the wall, a wave of ant–sized beasts. One super–sized one seemed to be leading the charge – they came one after another until around 100 of them were all in the room.

"What are these creatures?" Vagar squealed.

"Vintromech ants, Vagar," Mark replied. Rorwa's eyes lit up at the sight of bugs. She knew she could take care of them. These beasts had jaws as sharp as a human's and were coloured blue, with three sections and six legs, two per section: head, chest, and abdomen. Mark knew how venomous these were, but he was not afraid. Oddly, these bugs were incredibly intelligent for an ant species.

But, because the vintromech ants were clicking their jaws together and acting suspiciously, Mark decided to check their emotions just in case. He had once read a book about vintromech ants, and sent a searching pulse of magic towards them. He nearly fell over as the powerful magic showed him that the vintromechs weren't hostile. They were gravitating towards Rorwa because they sensed that she wasn't thinking any respectful thoughts about them and wanted to show her who's boss.

Vagar was practically hanging from the roof and whining like a child. Mark was simply standing in the corner whistling, trying to drown out Vagar. Rorwa was trapped in the centre on the verge of laughter. "They're not dangerous. Why don't you come down?" Mark asked Vagar. Vagar was about to shout abuse at Mark for suggesting such an idea. But just then the creaky door opened, revealing a bruised youth, his left eye surrounded by tiny scars. He was wearing a grey, long–sleeved shirt and coughing as if a desert had been crammed down his throat.

"Velostic, is that you?" asked Rorwa, looking at the young boy as if he was her own brother. Despite his young age, he had been a friend of hers back in the Templarian City, and they had fought in many battles together. She wondered how he had ended up here.

"Yes it's me," he said, lifting his foot to crush a bug.

"Don't. They won't hurt you," Mark said, placing a rugged hand on the newcomer's shoulder.

"Why shouldn't I?" asked Velostic, shrugging off the wizard's hand. Mark responded by jolting the child with blue energy.

"Did you just blast me with magic, little man," demanded the boy. His eyes seemed to turn as solid as ice and as hard as steel. He was just shorter than Vagar but no less intimidating.

"Yes kid, I did. They're not dangerous." Mark grunted, his voice quavering half–way through.

"Well, they could kill *me* in thirty milliseconds," he snarled, shoving Mark in the shoulder. Mark went for a swing but Velostic caught his hand, and held him against the wall by his throat. He could feel the air being squeezed out of him. Soon all Mark could see was black.

"Sir? Sirrrrr?" The emperor's personal worker was checking on her leader. The door had been locked for a while now. It had been fifteen minutes and the emperor had not responded.

She was worried. The emperor was never this quiet. At last she broke down the door and was appalled at what she saw. "Oh save me!" The emperor Sxxx the 223st was dead.

In the food processing centre, Arda was looking at his scanner. He saw some gooey juice in a fizzy drink. Usually humans like you and me would remove it quickly, close it down, and get the place fumigated and sprayed with disinfectant. But Arda just said, "Nutritious!" He left it inside and was about to move to the next bit of food, some liver, when there was an alarm.

BLOOO BLOOO BLOOO BLOOO BLOOOOOOO!

Arda threw the piece of liver at the alarm button. The alarm stopped and was replaced by a message from The Board of Basilisks. "Urgent! Urgent! Urgent! Urgent! Come to the Basilisk Assembly if you don't want to hear this message!" Arda didn't want to hear the message, so he went off.

A large dome with amethyst incrustations reflected the deep, purple light onto the central podium where the Councilor stood. In slithered Arda, among the other basilisks which were gathering around him. They came in from all for entrances, oriented towards the cardinal points. Each one of the doorways was set with their own stone: Ruby, Jade, Amber, and Sapphire.

All the basilisks stared up at the Councilor, wondering what had torn them away from their daily tasks. "I have sad news for you all." The Councilor's voice was deep and strong but was slightly raw – very out of ordinary for a basilisk. The Councilor never let his feelings show, whether on his face or in his voice.

"The Emperor is dead."

Back in the cell, Vagar looked around. The bugs were all gone. One moment they were covering Rorwa in what looked like a seething blanket, which clicked as the bugs clambered over each other, trying to get closer to Rorwa, then she said a word to them, and they were all gone like they'd never been there. "How did you do that?" asked Vagar.

"I don't know," she replied. They heard a slithering noise from outside and Rorwa stood up hastily. "Are they coming back?" Vagar asked. The cell door clattered open.

"You are wanted in the grand meeting room," hissed a silvery–scaled guard at the new prisoner. "Templarian, come with us."

Velostic recognized the guard's voice. "Sir – yes sir," he responded sarcastically. There were two guards waiting outside, and before he could speak any magic, they grabbed him by the arms and legs, and taped his mouth with a magic tape. Velostic could only muster out four words, 'Where are you taking –', before his mouth was shut. After that he could only scream against the tape.

They dragged him with harsh force. He wriggled but couldn't escape. The world turned black as they pulled a hood over his eyes. And then, when it was finally pulled off, there was nothing but a single light.

Arda hadn't been back to work for long when he heard yet another announcement. "The Grand Execution of the Templarian known as Velostic will be held at twelve–pm. Be there." Immediately, Arda ordered work to stop. He groaned, put down the food that he had been working on, and drove up to the main hall.

Velostic could hear the Basilisk voices gathering around him, chatting excitedly. All he could see was the bright light over his head. "I'll make a deal." A calm but distinct voice reached out to him, as if it was an old friend. "Just hold my hand, and I'll save you." Velostic reached out but there was nothing there. He realised, suddenly, that the voice was in his head. Someone was magically communicating with him using telepathy.

He knew that any moment, once the crowd had filled up, he would be injected with deadly basilisk poison. What could it be? Shashiminve, the poison that rots your face? Corevex, the deadly nerve agent? Raraçev, a deadly poison gas which infects the lungs? Or, Σneßchev, the one so deadly that even its true spelling is censored.

"My name…" the voice spoke out to him. He could now see a face floating up from his mind. "Is Clover." The vision faded away.

The crowd was now huge. They chanted and cheered. "*Kill him! Kill him! Kill him!*" Arda watched from the crowd, as the human was dragged up the stairs. He wasn't cheering. Velostic saw himself take the last steps up onto the execution platform, and before he could do anything, he was thrown onto the floor.

"Welcome, meek Templarian," the Councilor hissed. "To your end." A brightly coloured snake slithered towards Velostic. Its fangs dug into his skin. And after a few seconds, he started screaming.

But no sound came out of his mouth.

A tingle ran up his legs, and then his chest, and then it reached his neck. The executioner, robed in a black garment, grabbed a grand axe.

He swung the axe towards Velostic's neck, and then... Nothing.

Chapter 7

A New Emperor

The crowd roared as Velostic's body was taken away. With the enemy Templarian dealt with, and the first execution complete, it was time to continue with the ritual.

"The time has come!" cried the Councilor, holding up the trigonal tablet. The audience oohed curiously. "Oooh! Ahhh!"

"You can stop that!" shouted the Councilor. "Now as I was saying before I was so RUDELY INTERRUPTED..." He glared at the audience, who kept quiet. "The time has come... to choose a new leader by ritual!" The crowd cheered. 'I'll now pass over to the High Priest as I feel a bit embarrassed about being in front of an audience!" The Councilor slithered off quickly as the High Priest glared at him. As the leadership ritual required, the High Priest put the trigonal tablet inside a basilisk skull. It flashed briefly with a weird green light. He picked it up and showed it to the audience. Most of them had heard of this ritual, but few had ever seen it! The audience exclaimed, "Ooooooh!!"

"QUIET!" screamed the High Priest. The crowd went silent again. "The test is simple." The priest smiled a vicious grin, "The crystal tablet will decide the candidates' fates." The priest slid away with an incredible grandeur, with his robe swaying behind him.

The first candidate was named Fallavale, a tall creature who was as strong as at least the next ten basilisks. He was as tall as the stairs leading up to the crystal and could definitely take a punch. He touched the trigonal tablet and its crystal rippled, before finally lighting up.

Fallavale fell before the tablet. He bled rapidly, and could not physically survive long. Blood was leaking from his mouth and he was screaming in agony. He seemed to be stuck in a headlock by invisible arms, and there was nothing he could do. Despite Fallavale's physique, no-one could survive that. He let out one final scream before falling over backwards, lying with his eyes wide, his skin an unnatural colour. Finally, the corpse disintegrated into invisibly small pieces. The High Priest seemed incredibly amused. "Those who are not worthy shall not ever see the light of day again," he said.

There was another candidate, one who did not flinch at torture or suffering, one popular and respected basilisk with a hint of narcissism. His name was Veneno. "I, Veneno the Great, shall claim the throne to this fine realm of basilisks!" he called across the great assembly hall. As he yelled, a few basilisks slithered out in disgust, but many cheered wildly.

"Veneno, Veneno, Veneno!" the crowd chanted. The High Priest climbed further up the altar, and silenced the crowd's hissing with a flick of his tail.

"We will now check his worth with the trigonal tablet!" he yelled across the room. The room was yet again filled with the sound of the basilisks' excited hissing. The High Priest silenced the hall with another flick of his tail. He held the crystal up to the light, then shone the reflection at Veneno's head, right in between his eyes. The Great Snake Spirit, which had been trapped in the trigonal tablet, emerged and flew through the air, before wrapping itself around Veneno. A whispering sound filled Veneno's head, and then he fell unconscious in the spirit's grasp, unable to breathe. The spirit unwrapped itself from the body of Veneno. He fell motionless on the floor.

"The crystal finds him... Unworthy!" the High Priest declared. There was a combination of excited yeses, disappointed noes, and pained oohs. The High Priest pushed the body off stage. 'Anyway,' the High Priest said, "NEXT!"

Not far away, Rorwa, Mark, and Vagar were being marched down a hall. "I can't stand this underground serpent hell," raged Vagar. He would have levelled this place to the ground if he had his storm powers, but he hadn't felt well – this place made him feel weak, as if his strength was being sapped. His thought process was interrupted by the blunt end of a spear. Sweat dripped down his forehead. The further they went down the corridor, the hotter and louder it got. There was a stream of constant abuse from their guards.

"Stop poking me, or I'll shove that demonic stick down your slippery throat, you fork–tongued..." exclaimed Rorwa, but she was silenced by another thwack to the head. Soon the three of them could hear the roars from the Great Hall.

"The High Priest needs to speak to you," said a Lamian guard, throwing them violently forward.

"Ooh! Ow!" moaned Mark.

"Owww!" screamed Vagar, as annoying as usual. Mark and Rorwa had started walking up the steps into the Hall, but Vagar was having a tantrum. "Why is everyone against me!?" he screamed. "This prison is the worst! I will complain to the manager!" A Lamian guard reached into a barrel of basilisk food, and flung it at the Templarian to shut him up.

"Yuck!" moaned Vagar, spitting out the slime.

Mark tried to sneakily pull out his wand, but a guard stole it as they entered up into the hall. "Oi!" yelled Mark. "Give that back!" The basilisk didn't listen, and started playing magic tricks.

"Don't do anything right now," whispered Rorwa. "Just continue walking and don't make any eye–contact."

"What is this place?" Vagar's head was spinning with the noise from the crowd, the hall was vast and wide, with outcrops of bleak granite spiking down from the ceiling. Vagar was trembling with fear, yet he couldn't help but hold a little hint of awe and respect for the architects who had made this grand hall. It had been a while since the sort of grandeur like this place was seen by his eyes, and it did not disappoint. He was being dragged up the stairs, all while his beige–green eyes flickered around the vast chamber, but he did not seem to notice. He was in view of the crowd before he came to his senses.

Suddenly, with a burst of anger, Vagar leapt out of the custody of the guards and ripped a metal pipe from the wall. He flung himself towards the guards holding Rorwa captive, but he was no match for the improved physique of the basilisk guards and he was once again apprehended. The crowd cheered about the sudden excitement. The High Priest tried to calm them, but they could not be shushed.

"*Kill them! Kill them! Kill them!*" roared the crowd. Mark turned to their captors.

"Hang on a minute!" he said. "I thought the High Priest wanted to talk to us!"

"He does," smirked the guard. "He'll say hello, before you're sacrificed to the trigonal tablet. The election ritual requires three more sacrifices."

As Rorwa walked up the stone steps to the ritual platform, she thought of all the things she hadn't done in life: had a family, settled down, eaten a piece of cheese that she had been saving for her 30th birthday (it had seen better days).

She counted the steps: *one, two, three, four, five, six, seven, eight, nine, ten, eleven, twelve, thirteen...* She had never liked the number thirteen. Even though she understood it was probably just a superstition, she still felt wary of the number the human race considered unlucky. She didn't get to finish her thoughts – the basilisk guard shoved her forward and she fell hard upon the stone altar.

Vagar had already been chained up at the top of the stairs. The smell of sweat and blood filled Rorwa's senses. Even though they argued sometimes, they were friends, and had fought by each other's side for years. After his escape attempt, the guards were being much stricter with him. The executioner had already raised his axe.

"Rorwa, I hope to see you in whatever place we go to next," Vagar cried, lowering his head. But a yell distracted them. The crystal's colour had changed. The crowd were silenced, all watching like hawks, staring at the red glow of crystal.

"This can't be happening," the High Priest cried. "*Noooooooo!*" His sly grin melted off his face like a lolly in the middle of the summer. "This can't be!" The High Priest stood in shock, caught up in his own power, he hadn't sensed that Rorwa had the qualities of the true heir. Vagar and Rorwa watched the tablet glow, but had no idea what it meant.

"Rorwa," Mark whispered. "I read this book about Basilisk Rituals, and it said that the tablet shines red when it meets the person that's perfect to become Emperor..." His voice faded away. He was trembling with excitement. "Or...Empress!" he finished proudly. The Executioner dropped his axe. Vagar was still screaming as if he was hitting the high note in a song.

Rorwa looked at the High Priest, who was looking back at her with fear and awe. "I think that the tablet has made me Empress," hissed Rorwa, looking around at the Basilisks.

"Well, make a big acceptance speech then!" replied Vagar. He had calmed down as soon as the Executioner had untied him, and was smiling as if the Basilisks had given him a drug that made him go crazy.

"Great Empress, what is your first order?" asked the Councilor, shouldering the High Priest out of the way. The other snake slithered away, grumbling to himself. Rorwa felt herself begin to smile.

Somewhere else, deep within the caves of the Crystal Caverns, the being called Clover wove a thread of magic, thin as a hair yet as complex as any fine lace. He stabbed the chicken and let its blood pour onto the altar. Tradition decreed he should use a human but a chicken would do just as well and Clover didn't like unnecessary waste. Smoke rose from the cold altar, it darkened and coalesced into an almost human form. "Velostic..." Clover hissed.

Velostic's deep purple eyes flickered open. His neck was still screaming in pain from the damage which was inflicted by the axe which had cut off his head. He scrambled up from the hard stone floor which, unfortunately for him, was boiling hot. The heat made him feel nauseous. Flashing lights blinded his vision. He stood up, or rather hovered to his feet, for the lack of a better word.

"Hello my friend. I have been expecting you." The voice which had moments ago filled his head now seemed to fill the room, echoing around the chamber and adding to his head-ache. Although it was warm and friendly, there was a cold, hard tone underneath it. Well disguised as that cold tone was, it was still quite obvious to Velostic. As he spun on the spot, his ghostly body felt infinitely strange–it didn't move, but his head went all the way around.

His new "friend" was a tall man with strangely white hair and bloody, red eyes that made him feel sick. His gut wrenched painfully. His body seemed to want to vomit. He was sure that, moments ago, it had been spilled all over the basilisk's Great Hall. His guts were about to be consumed by some snakes. His throat was filled by an acidic feeling.

"Trust me, I am not your friend," he grunted."What have you done to me?"

"I have saved you," said Clover. "I saved you from being killed by the basilisks. Well, you were killed, technically." He smiled cheekily at Velostic.

"Don't be stupid," Velostic hissed. "What do you mean?"

"Your body has died. It is still in the Great Hall, where it is probably being eaten as we speak." Velostic felt sick to hear the man say this. "But I have saved your spirit. You live on as a shade."

"What if I don't want to be a shade?" replied Velostic. "I'd rather be dead than do your bidding."

Clover twirled his fingers, casting yellow magic, which tied up Velostic's arms and legs. He found himself walking across the room. Clover smiled. "You haven't got any other choice."

Chapter 8

The Five New Laws

Back in the Great Hall, Rorwa stood before the thousands of serpent faces looking up at her. "No, I cannot be the emperor," she said finally, looking through the gigantic crowd for a worthy basilisk. But she found no-one. "I have to get back to the Templarians. I only have enough time for one job, not one job and the ruling of a huge kingdom of a species I am not a part of."

Vagar looked at Rorwa like she was a raving idiot.

"Rorwa!" he whispered angrily, "If you don't accept the position, we'll be tortured until our last breath! You must accept this!"

She couldn't argue with that, so she reluctantly agreed, before being led into a meeting room with a council waiting.

A basilisk slithered slowly and deliberately into the dark, misty room. He paused for a minute and stretched for a bit and moaned. He set himself down in his stone seat and spoke very slowly, "My... name... is... Slithery... Slither..." he began. "The... oldest... basi... lisk... on... this... planet... Now... what... rules... would... you... like... to... make...?" Slithery's question came out so slowly that it was practically impossible for anyone else to concentrate. Mark and Vagar were snoring by the time he'd finished his sentence. "Honk...Shoo...honk... shooooooo!"

"What are you two playing at?" moaned Rorwa. "'Honk shoo?' You sound like a pair of shoe horns!"

Slithery put his tentacle across the table and handed her a piece of paper slowly. It would have taken almost three days. Rorwa was exasperated. She just snatched the piece as it was a quarter of a way across the table.

"Emperors... don't... snaaaaaaaaaaattcccchh!" rumbled Slithery. Rorwa didn't care. She read it through. She almost fainted when she handed it back. "Ssssssssso?" asked Slithery.

After some time they made their way back into the hall.

It rose high above them, its roof a distant blur. Sometimes, the older basilisks thought they saw clouds at the top of it, obscuring the large diamond set into the centre of the dome, which would project sunlight from the outside world onto any speaker stood on the central podium, bathing them like a spotlight. Rorwa could now see the hall itself more clearly than before. It was a large stone chamber with four doors oriented towards the cardinal directions: North, East, South, West. Each door was framed in stones, four different gemstones for the four different portals. North had Sapphire, South had Ruby, West had Emerald and East had Topaz. The four colours would bathe their respective quarters in a dim light. It was a perfect way to split the groups. The red Ruby segment was for the military, the blue Sapphire was for the priests and their apprentices, yellow Topaz was for the miners, and green Emerald was for everyone else. The floor flagstones were set with iridescent, semi-transparent stones that made it look as though the basilisks were slithering on shining mist. Sometimes basilisks said they saw shapes in the misty ground; the priests thought it told the future and could spend hours staring into the iridescent depths. The only thing they had predicted so far was lunch. But they and the apprentices were making progress – they thought that they might be up to predicting breakfast soon!

The note that Slithery had given to her had made it all clear. Rorwa needed to come up with five brand new laws if she was to be accepted as Empress, as the rituals required. But she looked out at the eager faces of the snakes as they bowed to her, and her mind went completely blank.

"I don't have any ideas, have you got any?" asked Rorwa shrugging.

"Yes!" answered Mark and Vagar almost in unison. The three of them retreated to the back of the podium to discuss it. When they had finished talking, Rorwa stood up and relayed what they had come up with.

"First: no more restrictions on magic, so that me and my allies can protect you and your families," declared Rorwa to the assembly, from the top of the massive platform.

"How do we know that you won't fry somebody?" asked somebody in the crowd. This unfortunate individual was on the end of a very grumpy Vagar, who used his newly restored magical powers to fry the serpent into a poor pile of ash.

"I told you he would use some very strange magic to kill some dude, as soon as he got the chance," said one of the guards that had brought the two destructive Templarian field commanders in, turning to his friend. "Maybe we're not so different after all!"

"If you don't comply with the Empress' rule then either I, or my new best friends, these guards, will kill you," announced Vagar, waving at the basilisks. The guards who knew nothing of this fact were confused, and then completely delighted when Vagar leant in, and told them they'd receive their brand new tail armour and poisoned tipped tridents for free!

"Secondly," Rorwa stated. "Humans shall be allowed to take political posts!" Mark and Vagar's ears pricked up at this. "My large friend here shall become the Councilor'" she said, pointing at Vagar, who was grinning from ear to ear. "And Mark here shall be the High Priest."

At this news many of the basilisks in the crowd started hissing evilly. The old Councilor and High Priest slithered off into the darkness. Mark whispered into Rorwa's ear. "Maybe no human eating? I don't want to be eaten as soon as your time as Empress runs out."

"Um, yeah, sure. Good idea I guess." She turned back to the crowd. "Basilisks! From now on there is to be no eat–"

"*Consumption,*" whispered Mark into her ear.

"Consumption," she agreed, "of any humans, whatsoever." She thought for a moment, then added, "unless the human started it." The basilisk faces were confused and angry. "Basically if a human tries to eat you, you can eat him. Not otherwise."

Many of the more important nobles were already planning out how to make it look like a human had tried to eat them. But other basilisks, chiefly Arda, had other things to worry about. "How will we stay strong if we only have porridge and carrots to eat!" he said. "How will I feed my customers without good food?"

The basilisk horde seethed and Rorwa seemed to be in danger, until Mark stepped up.

"Bring in the cow!"

A cow was dragged in, frantically mooing and dragging at the rope which the basilisks were dragging it by. "This is what you will eat from now on," proclaimed Mark grandly. The basilisks calmed down a little.

"It looks disgusting though," one of the younger serpents exclaimed. The muttering started again. Thankfully, Mark saved the day again.

"Bring in the cooked cow meat!"

That silenced the basilisks. In seconds they had emptied the trays that were brought in and were contentedly wishing for more. "This stuff is the best. Maybe an alien Empress isn't so bad after all!" remarked one of them.

"Cows will be supplied to the head cook. Oops, sorry. The head food producer." Arda slithered reluctantly up to the stage. Rorwa kept going with the speech but no one was really listening anymore. It had been a huge success. "Perhaps we can change something else," she muttered. Arda looked as if he was about to murder her. "We might change the chocolate as well, it's unhygienic," sniffed Rorwa.

Arda sighed and agreed, but as soon as she was out of ear-shot, he turned to the basilisk beside him. "Huh, what does she want next?" he said. "My slime stores?"

"The fourth law shall be that no one shall try to overthrow the Empress. And the fifth and final law is... all money should be collected and shared with the less fortunate!" announced Rorwa. Vagar grimaced at this announcement, but he said nothing. He wasn't about to argue with the Empress in front of all her subjects and their sharp teeth.

"You what! Why? No!" All the rich basilisks started to hiss aggressively towards Rorwa. The poor basilisks started to cheer for her in appreciation. Both sides of the hall had different thoughts about the five new laws.

"Every single penny that you have needs to be with me within a couple of days, or else!" shouted Rorwa over the disagreement that was happening between two groups of basilisks.

"You don't deserve the money that we have earnt!" hissed a noble basilisk.

"Hiss you don't deserve money at all, you spoiled basilisks!" replied a poor basilisk.

"Everybody, silence! If you do not agree to these laws you will be punished severely!" bellowed Rorwa. The vast hall fell as silent as a graveyard. Nothing could be heard.

Slowly, the meeting came to an end, and the basilisks made

their way out of the hall, either grumbling or whispering excitedly.

"These basilisk nobles do not like the idea of giving up their money," said Mark, watching them slither out. "Maybe there will be a revolt?"

"We need to execute the nobles!" Vagar cried as he smashed his chain mailed fist onto the wooden table, nearly cracking the crystal. His desire to kill overpowered his thoughts about the law. "If they think we are soft they will strike."

"We can't just execute a bunch of important basilisks without evidence," protested Rorwa.

Mark sided with her. "Basilisks would attack a cruel and unjust ruler even quicker than a weak one."

"Ah well," Vagar said angrily. "I won't be around when they turn on you." He stomped out of the room. Rorwa and Mark exchanged glances, then followed behind.

Chapter 9

The Basilisk Revolt

By that evening they had managed to get Vagar to calm down, and had met up again in the Empress' Chamber to discuss the problem. Rorwa found herself tired, almost falling asleep, arguing with Vagar about the basilisks. "We need to convince them to follow the new laws," she said. "They already seem to have calmed down!"

"That's what they want you to think," spat Vagar. "They want you to put your guard down!"

Rorwa was about to retort, when she realised she could sense something in the corner of the room. The curtain which hung there was flickering, but there wasn't any wind. As Vagar was talking, she crept up to it, then looked around it and gasped.

"A SPY!" she yelled.

"A SPY! A SPY!" screamed Vagar and Mark. They leapt at the shadow and smashed into the wall.

"OW!" groaned Vagar.

"That's only the spy's shadow, you morons, the spy was over there!" sighed Rorwa. She pointed at another ledge, then went after the spy and pinned him down.

"GET OFF ME!" he screamed.

"I recognise you," said Rorwa, flashing her torch at Arda's slimy face. "You were at the election!"

"Yes, I am Arda – head of the food processing centre," he said. "I love what you did with the food! I would like to help you escape here and get you back to your city!" Rorwa got off the slimy basilisk. Mark and Vagar stumbled over.

"Didja geddhim?" mumbled Vagar as one of his front teeth fell out. Mark cast a spell and put it back in his mouth. "Thanks!" smiled Vagar. "Can you cast a spell to make my teeth permanently clean?"

"We must leave now," Arda said, not at all close to a joking tone. "I've come to warn you that I overheard the nobility planning a revolt."

"What!?" Rorwa was shocked. "This can't be!" Her eyes were sad. Her new laws had seemed like such a great idea, but a perfect idea on the surface always fell apart the more you thought about it.

"It can, cause that's what's happening right now," Arda stared intently at Rorwa.

"Well, we must strike first, we should execute them all!" Vagar advised.

"No, they are more powerful than you would know." Arda looked disappointed. "We must escape."

The group paused and exchanged glances, portraying unspoken words, and holding their torches. "But how can we trust you?" Mark asked the worker.

"Because I've been looking for an opportunity to escape." Mark quietly cast a spell to check the basilisk's emotions and saw that he was telling the truth. He nodded wearily to the other two Templarians. "There are three particular nobles who want revenge." Arda knew what he was doing. "Savalch Kekolu, Sirin Kchorlia, and the most feared military general, Meneravchiiyn Berli."

"Ok, fine, fine, fine," Rorwa sighed. "But first we need to find Velostic. He was taken from our cell before us. We need to bring him with us if we're going to escape."

Arda looked at her, sadly. "Do you mean the young Templarian, with purple eyes?"

"Yes," Rorwa said. "How can we get to him?"

Arda wasn't sure what to say, so Mark spoke for him. "They killed him, didn't they? He was executed before we got there." Arda didn't reply, but his face said everything. Rorwa felt like crying but wiped away her tears.

"He was a strong warrior," she said. "He died like a Templarian should." She felt Vagar's comforting hand touch her shoulder, but shrugged it away. "Now how do we get out of this place?" She paused. "Before they get us, preferably."

"This way," Arda said, slithering away. The three Templarians looked at each other, then followed after.

Meanwhile, the basilisk nobility were hard at work on their plans for the coup, just as Arda had warned. Savalch stood above the map of the basilisk kingdom, along with Sirin and

Meneravchiiyn.

"Meiiyn, do you know of any more options they have to escape?" Sirin spoke in a deep voice.

"No, no way. I've worked with every escape route in this kingdom for 15 years," she responded. "There could be one in the southern area, but those people fear me more than death."

"Savalch?" Sirin asked.

"There is a singular escape in my palace, but no-one would be stupid enough to break into my castle," Savalch stated proudly. "The castle that I wouldn't need to arm if it wasn't for this horrid leader," he shouted.

"Woah, woah." Meneravchiiyn, or as everyone close to her called her, Meiiyn, tried to calm him down. "Anyway, Sirin, have you got any escape routes to patch?"

"Hahahaha," Sirin laughed. "As if."

"When will your soldiers reach the Empress?" Meiiyn asked.

"Any second now," smirked Sirin.

He was right. They met the Templarians just as they left Rorwa's chamber. Sirin's soldiers charged forward, easily recognisable by the red plumes they wore on their heads. It wasn't a particularly smart idea to show off the fact that you were a traitor but noble basilisks had never been too intelligent. Swords bounced off the scales and the group retreated.

"This calls for magic," Mark announced and threw fireballs at the advancing horde, while the rest managed to slip by the basilisks into the tunnels.

"This way!" hissed Arda. The basilisks tried to pursue them but were stopped in their tracks by Mark's flames. The marble sized fireballs seared holes into the basilisks' scales, going through armour and thick skin alike, incinerating the basilisks from the inside. A few seconds later only a burnt skeleton was left lying in a puddle of melted iron and carapace. The basilisks turned back and hid behind a burnt column. They needed reinforcements, particularly archers. The basilisks waited, and so did Mark.

Deeper into the tunnels, Vagar stumbled into a giant pipe and walked along its walkway. Arda was in front, with Rorwa and Vagar following close behind. Having left Mark alone with the soldiers, Vagar was starting to feel very scared. Rorwa sighed. "Vagar," she said. "Why are you moaning like this? You were basically a guy that rushes into battles and isn't scared of anything! Except bees."

"W–w–w–w–w–" stammered Vagar.

"W–w–w–w–w–w–what?" groaned Rorwa, starting to get annoyed.

"W–w–w–WE SHOULD GO AND GET MARK!" screamed Vagar. His voice echoed against the tunnels.

"SHHHHH!" shushed Arda. "Why? It's a suicide mission!"

"Alright, I'll get him!" announced Vagar, and broke away from the crowd.

Mark suddenly felt a lurch in his head. He retreated behind a column as the basilisks started advancing again. His mana reserve had run out and needed time to regenerate, time he didn't have. If he persisted in casting spells using his aura, every spell would drain his reserves. He pulled out an artifact he always brought with him on missions, calling upon its powers. Everything around him start to swirl. Suddenly blue clouds thickened, and then a carriage emerged from them, pulled by a ghost–like horse. He used his last drop of power to dive into the carriage, which flew out and carried him into the spirit dimension.

Vagar was running down the tunnel when he heard angry shouting behind him. It was the basilisk guards! Then he came upon a crossroads of sewer pipes. Crouching low in the shadows, he hid behind a corner and the clueless guards ran past him. "Where can Mark be?" he wondered to himself. Then a figure put his hand on Vagar's shoulder. "HA ARRRRRGGGGGHHH!" he screamed. Horrified, he drew his sword.

"Jeez, Vagar!" moaned Mark, clutching his sore head. "I feel dizzy. I've obviously had a nightmare or something. I've been to a different dimension."

Vagar could still see the blue clouds swirling around Mark, and saw the carriage made of smoke disappearing down the tunnel. "Well, you weren't dreaming, Mark," he sighed. The two walked off down the walkway and met Rorwa and Arda.

"Where have you two been?" asked Rorwa.

"We've almost had a heart attack!" cried Arda.

"You didn't have a heart attack when Mark was almost taken prisoner," retorted Vagar.

"Come on, let's go," sighed Mark. With that, they walked off down the sewage walkway and off to their next destination.

Chapter 10

Snakes and Ladders

The four adventurers wandered aimlessly for a long time, looking for their way out. "Are we sure this hatchling knows what he's doing?" asked Vagar. Rorwa ignored him.

Suddenly, Arda remembered something. "Hey!" he exclaimed. "Come down here! I know where to find another way." Following Arda, they climbed down into a secret tunnel that even the guards didn't know about, hidden behind an iron grate. When they reached the end of the hidden passage there was a tube facing upwards and disappearing into the ceiling. Inside it was a rusty ladder, and looking upwards they could see a tiny dot of light, far above them. "Here it is," said Arda. "The way back to the surface. This is how the smugglers get in and out." Mark and Vagar didn't need to hear anything else, and wrestled each other to be the first up the ladder. The other two followed behind. They climbed for what felt like hours, but at last reached the top, and found themselves in what looked to be a vast desert, great, yellow sands spreading out in every direction. Luckily for them, some smuggler had left a Dune Rider next to the exit–a yellow painted, rusty hunk of metal, only a bit bigger than a motorcycle, but designed specifically to cross the sand at top speed. It had a silver 098 printed on the side, and the handles on the front were made of rubber and metal. As they were about to climb up, Rorwa looked over to Arda, who sighed.

"Arda, come with us!" she cried.

"No, you go on without me." sighed Arda. They could hear two basilisks yelling at the bottom of the tube; it wouldn't be long before they reached the top!

"Go, Rorwa! Go back to your people! I'll escape!"

"But... but..." stammered Rorwa, tears welling in her eyes.

Vagar was halfway through the dune rider window (there's no point in using a door if there is a window), when Mark pulled him back. "We can't just leave Arda here without any powers or way of asking for help – the nobility will definitely kill him, forget Rorwa's laws, seize power, and everything would be back to the way it was before – minus Arda."

Mark whispered to Rorwa, who smiled and nodded. He gave the Empress a scroll and quill, which she quickly wrote a carefully worded message onto, then signed at the bottom. Mark handed Arda the scroll.

"This makes you king of the basilisks until further notice. Basically you're king now, your majesty." He gave a mock bow.

"What?" asked Arda, wide-eyed.

Rorwa smiled and linked hands with Mark, who stepped towards Arda and put a hand on his forehead. Arda felt a chill through his body and his tiredness fall away.

"Nothing too overpowered," Rorwa explained apologetically. "Hardened scales – to make sure you don't die from assassins, sharper fangs – to make sure you can deal with said assassins, more stamina – so you have the tirelessness necessary for a ruler, more intelligence – you are already smart, but being a bit more smart is always good when you're dealing with nobles and their plots." Throughout the entire lecture, Arda was stood with his yellow eyes wide. This was more than he had ever expected. There was still even more to come.

"Well, we can't just leave you without any way to ask for help. So take this device," Mark said, passing a strange object to Arda.

"What is this?" Arda pondered, confused about what he had just been given.

"It's an Aligned Lodestone System, one of the newest ones," Mark explained. "It allows instant communication from any distance, up to 25 Eseni's."

"Wow," Arda was shocked at the kindness. He was not used to it. "You humans really don't have to help me."

"Yes we do," Rorwa stated, not open to hearing the other side of the story. "If we don't help you, you'll end up being processed for food in your own processing plant!"

"Here, this is a magic bracelet. I imbued it with some of my powers," muttered Vagar as he gave him a bracelet. He shook the serpent's hand and patted him on the back.

"Thank you," muttered Arda."What does it do?"

"It shoots thousands of bolts of lighting at once," said Vagar, nodding, before walking off.

"Okay," the basilisk smiled. "Great."

"What are you going to do?" asked Rorwa. "The nobles aren't going to make you king just because I said so. They're in the middle of chasing me out of the kingdom!"

"I'll have to prove myself to them," he said, sternly. "It's okay, I know the basilisks, I've been feeding some of the nobles since they were hatchlings! I'll be able to convince them." He looked down at the weapons and new powers he had been given. "And besides, I'll be the strongest of them now," he smiled. "And I don't have the problem of being a human."

"True," Rorwa agreed. But before they could wish him well, they heard the soldiers start climbing up the bottom of the ladder. Before they knew it, Arda was conjuring lightning with Vagar's bracelet and diving back down the tunnel.

"Well, no time to waste," Rorwa exclaimed, hopping into the dune rider. It was very cramped inside with the three of them. Arda wouldn't have fit anyway. She put her foot on the pedal: it was shiny and cold, unlike the rest of the Dune Rider. The Dune Rider was very responsive, despite how old it looked, and it shot off away from the basilisk cave. The sunlight was bright in their eyes, but they could not have been happier.

After some hours of flying away from the basilisk territory, they stopped to think about what to do next. Rorwa jumped out of their vehicle and idly raised a large stone out of the ground, throwing it against a giant mountain, making it shatter into tiny fragments. Vagar was always impressed by how powerful she could be.

"What do we do next," roared Rorwa as she continued to use her levitation powers to entertain herself by breaking boulders.

"We could just go back to the order," suggested Mark, as he sat down near a rock.

"What, you want Yshkavis to catch us again, and feed us to Ikari?" scoffed Vagar. "I don't think so."

"Shut up! Where are we going to go if not to the Templarians?" grunted Rorwa, shoving both of them.

"I'm not going back to prison. The Templarians will never welcome us back. You know that," said Vagar. "We have two options. Either A, we camp out in the Oxtaverde Woods and find some decent food, or B, you two leave me behind."

The group was silent. They could see the tops of the trees just over the horizon. The Templar City lay beyond the forest, anyway. There wouldn't be any way around.

"He's right," Mark said at last, reluctantly. "It's not a risk worth taking."

"Well what do you suggest then, Mark?" Rorwa was annoyed, now. "Sit in the forest for the rest of our lives?"

"Why don't you suggest something? I thought you were the Great Empress?" Mark snapped.

"Mark, you are about as much use as a chocolate teapot," Rorwa retorted.

"Well, maybe if you listened to me, I wouldn't have to be snarky!" he shouted.

"You love being the centre of the universe don't you? Well I have a reality check for you. You aren't!" Rorwa screamed back.

"You know what," Vagar was trembling. "I've had enough of you two. I'm going to the forest to find food, and I don't care if you follow me!"

With that he stormed off. Mark was happy enough to follow behind. Rorwa was annoyed, but decided to go with them. She knew that on the other side of the forest was the Templar City, and that once they'd been able to regain their strength, she might be able to convince them to return.

As they journeyed into the forest, not one of them noticed the hooded figure following them, treading silently through the dark…

Chapter 11

A Haunted Forest

The trio walked under the everlasting canopy of the Oxtaverde Woods. The trees stretched higher than some mountains but the leafy expanse started surprisingly low down. The larger part of the trees was a knotted mess of branches bound together by fleshy green vines and covered by wide leaves that, unlike most trees, were not used to collect sunlight. Since, even if you got above the canopy, the lush climate resulted in many clouds, the trees collected water to survive. As the water poured down through the leafy expanse, the bucketfuls of water were slowly absorbed, but not straight away–every leaf took a few droplets until the flow dwindled to a trickle, and only minuscule droplets reached the trio. Mark gathered berries and fruits that he knew from his studies were safe to eat, and the group ate quietly as they wandered through the vast forest.

"I don't like this." Vagar muttered, as reluctant as any of them to disrupt the fragile yet majestic silence with loud voices. "A big tree will definitely have big parasites. And if we have any hope of making it through here alive…"

"Can you sense any insects here Rorwa?" Mark asked.

"It's strange, there are no insects here, only strange arachnids. It feels wrong somehow. It's almost like a spider except it feels big, and negatively attuned to travellers."

Mark and Vagar looked at each other.

"Giant spider?!?"

When the giant spiders leapt down at them Mark was ready with his fireballs. Vagar sliced the few that got too close, while Rorwa still vainly tried to establish contact with the enormous beasts. They didn't seem interested in communicating with her in the way bugs normally were.

"This is too easy," Vagar panted. "They shouldn't die that easily. My sword is going through them as though they weren't there." He paused when he saw Mark, who wasn't sending fireballs any longer, but soon enough he was back to batting off the poisonous spiders with his sword.

Velostic slipped through the bushes, cloaked in shadows. As a shade he didn't rustle a twig. He cast the same spell over and over again, as he had been ordered. Fooled by Clover's mastery of illusions, the trio, who didn't yet know they were being watched, fought the ferocious spiders. Velostic melted away, there was no danger of them catching him. He would have liked to finish them off. His thoughts had somehow twisted into a new shape and he was feeling murderous towards his old peers. His orders were different now, and he couldn't disobey orders – he thought that at least was normal. He flew swiftly through the trees. Now Velostic's body was dead and gone, and although he hated being a ghost, his new master knew he could do more damage in his shadow form.

The wizard was watching the spiders intently. As Vagar and Rorwa dealt with the onslaught, they noticed the corpses of the spiders faded away into smoke. What Vagar and Rorwa hadn't realised (Vagar had been too busy with his sword and Rorwa with her insect tricks) was the necrotic residue that the spiders were leaving behind. They were a sign of undead creatures, who had been brought to life by a necromancer. Mark began to realise that the spider attack was the work of dark magic.

Out of the corner of his eye Mark saw a figure lurking in the trees. Mark was still battling the ghostly spiders, so it was hard to keep track of it. He fought one off and pinned it against a tree, shoving another down with a sharp branch. When he escaped, Mark rushed over to where Velostic had just been, but he was furious because the mysterious stranger had disappeared! Frustrated, he returned to the others. The spider attack was over.

"Guys, take a look at this," Mark said. He tried but couldn't determine the magic 'fingerprint' of the mage who had cast the spell. The only hints that the spiders had ever existed were the scratches which everyone had received. They weren't deep wounds, Vagar had grazed himself harder when falling on a rock but Mark insisted upon healing everyone anyway, as he knew they were probably laced with poison. They would need to all link their abilities to heal each other. Mark chanted a healing spell, whilst Rorwa and Vagar concentrated on making it stronger with their insect and grey storm powers combined.

Poison was already hard to heal, and magic poison was very hard. In terms of magic ability, you had to be within a narrow margin of the mage who had cast it and, for all the group knew, that could have been anyone!

"I seriously think that it's our duty to inform the Order about everything that's happened, Arda might have trouble with the angry basilisk nobles," said Rorwa, thinking aloud.

"Agreed, but I'm more worried about this new threat – whoever is casting dark magic," replied Mark. Exchanging nervous looks and nods, the trio realised that for once they were in agreement.

"Whoever cast the spell on those spiders, it's very likely that they put sentries in the forest," said Vagar. The others nodded and hoped that their powers had been enough to heal their poisoned scratches. They rested a bit to regain their magic reserve and then kept going. They had to reach the city urgently.

Far away, a strange white haired figure watched over the forest, sensing a loss. Likely Clover knew that his spiders had been destroyed, and maybe even knew the Templarians' faces now. He had sent his new shade accomplice, Velostic, into the forest to find the group and torment them on their journey.

It was a wary party that kept going along the path, and they all kept their senses at the peak for the rest of the journey

"If there are any spiders left, catch them alive." Rorwa said quietly. "I think I've worked out a way to make one do what I want. And what I want is answers."

"It might be too late for that," replied Mark, "We should be keeping an eye out for the mage who was casting spells against us!"

Waste of time, Vagar thought, *whoever he or she was had a very long time to run away.* But when Rorwa gathered them together to cast a locater charm, he didn't say a thing against it. After all, magic could always do better than eyes – but nobody could beat some of the most powerful mages still alive when they linked together.

Velostic, travelling silently through the trees in ghost form, had returned to following the others. Half-heartedly, he passed through the bushes. He still wasn't too keen on obeying Clover. Suddenly he was exposed – Mark and Rorwa's charm was channelling light towards him!

"There he is!" shouted Mark, lunging towards him. He caught up to the silent cloaked man, but as he grabbed him a gust of wind passed, and the only thing Mark was left with was an empty cloak.

Velostic sighed with relief as he disappeared into the shadowy forest. He knew soon enough they would discover the illusion, and Rorwa, Vagar and Mark would uncover his betrayal. But that didn't matter. He had a new master now.

Chapter 12

A Ghost on the Throne

Somewhere in the Templarian City was a chamber. It was almost pitch black. The room was only lit by a small candle. Everyone was there because they were holding elections for the new leader of the order. As usual, the election started with a speech. "Ladies and gentlemen!" began the vice–grandmaster. "We'll start with the speech of the Order!" And with that, he started jabbering away for what seems like hours. After two minutes, he was hooked off the stage. So the first person went up to the stage.

"Hello, everyone," he announced. "My name is ..."

"What?" asked a man in the crowd.

"It's ..."

"What?"

"..."

The man whose name was the three dots man went on and on. After ten minutes he was chased off the stage by rotten banana peels and tomatoes. Then the second nominee stepped up.

"My name is Moonman. I would like to say that I'm going to make biiiiiig changes!"

"GET HIM OFF THE STAGE!" yelled another man. The crowd all booed him and he was chased off the stage.

"I'LL BE BACK!" he bellowed, and trudged off.

Then the third nominee stepped up. He had a black cloak draped up on his head. So no one could see his face. It was Velostic. He gave a big and powerful speech that included some words that cannot be said. It ended with a round of applause.

"YES!" cried the first man.

"HE'S OUR NEW GRANDMASTER!" called the woman beside him.

A few minutes later, everyone voted at the polling station, and out of all the three nominees, Velostic was the one everyone voted for. Well, mostly. The three dots man got one vote. He voted for himself.

In the large square outside the chamber, the major political elite of the Order were gathered, waiting for the new Grandmaster, mixed in with all the other citizens of Templarian City, as was tradition. The large balcony, on which the new leader would be announced, was empty. The people had been standing out for hours; the nice eighteen–degree heat was not too hot, there were barrels of ale being sold and steaks being roasted. There had been a time of great economic growth in the city, but there was a sad atmosphere. Soon everyone would sit down and sing mourning songs. It had been two months since the old master's death, and the Templarians were still mourning. Everyone was on high alert, as the military presence needed to keep order in the city had left the borders open to attack. The months since the Grandmaster's death had seen a lot of the elites quickly lose their hair.

"I wonder who it will be?" said Blooble to his brother as he placed his hand on his bishop checking his brother king.

"I'm betting on …, the commander of the northern armies," responded Nooble as he took the bishop and placed it on the side. They looked out of the open window of their incredibly expensive house, which Blooble bought after winning the Templarian lottery. Nooble had, surprisingly, had a very pleasant time since he had returned to the Templar City. Blooble had been able to buy his brother's freedom with some of his winnings, on the condition that Nooble never served in the Templarian army again, and kept his head down until the end of his sentence. This suited Nooble rather well. No one paid him any attention, with the danger of the basilisks and the recent death of the old Grandmaster on everyone's minds. Blooble had just advised him not to let his freedom be known to Yshkavis, who would surely kill him if she caught him, whether the other Templarians liked it or not.

Sadly, the Templarians hadn't cared much when he'd told them that the basilisks had captured Rorwa and Vagar. Actually, they just laughed. "Let them try and escape," the vice–grandmaster had said to him. "They always acted like they were so powerful! Let's see them prove it."

The two brothers heard a trumpet sound distantly, along

with the cheer of a crowd. "Come on, Nooble," Blooble said. "Put your hood on, and let's go and find out who our new leader is."

They arrived in the square just in time to see Velostic up on the balcony above the enormous crowd, as the vice–grandmaster crowned him! Blooble knelt to praise his new leader. Nooble just stood looking at him, before Blooble yanked him down to his knees. He thought there was something strange about the new Grandmaster, something that he recognised…

Chapter 13

An Unfriendly City and a Surprise Reunion

After trudging for hours through the forest, they emerged, and saw at last the beautiful white walls looming over them, the seldom–seen city of the Templarians concealed inside. Rorwa, Vagar and Mark looked at it warily. It was safe from spiders but a shade, as they suspected their new enemy was, could easily slip through the thick walls, passing between the pointed battlements without alerting the archers. The walls could stop anything, from flames, to tornadoes, to catapults – but nothing like that.

They arrived at the city gates, but as they tried to walk through, the three were kicked out, literally. Rorwa rubbed her back and stood up; a guard's footprint was left in the middle of her chest where she had been booted.

"You are fugitives, and you are no longer welcome in the Templarian City," sounded a booming voice from a high up battlement, "Try to enter again and you will be arrested, or worse!"

"This has gone too far!" she cried. "The knights have never kicked us out!" The group were enraged. After all they had done, and how far they had come, they couldn't bear the idea that they were being rejected by the Order. Something didn't feel right "This is WAR!" Rorwa shouted, and the others drew their weapons following her lead.

They began to charge at the gates, then stopped when Vagar asked, "Shouldn't we sit this one out and figure out a logical idea to get inside without killing ourselves?" Rorwa stopped herself and Mark.

"Vagar's right." sighed Rorwa. "We should find a logical way to get inside."

"I have an idea!" cried Mark. "Let's go to the side entrance of the city! Only I know the way in. The guards haven't found out yet! Let's go!" They ran back through the forest for quite a while, but soon, they got tired.

"Huh, huh, huh!" moaned Rorwa, gasping for breath. "How long until we get to the entrance, Mark?"

"I dunno!" cried Mark, it was starting to become dark. "We should find a place to sleep."

Soon they had found a place to sleep – an old camping tent. The three fell asleep almost immediately, and slept for a good four hours or so, when they were woken up by grunting and rustling. Rorwa and Mark got up suddenly. They got out their swords and looked around. Then a twig snapped and two shadowy figures thrust towards the two. The foremost had a glint of yellow and was completely covered by a robe. He took it off. It was Nooble!

"Huh, huh!" he panted, exhausted from his attempt to warn his friends. He was desperate to help them as they had helped him all that time ago, when he was down on his luck in prison.

"Nooble!" exclaimed Rorwa. "How've you been?" She was amazed to see him, having assumed he'd perished in an unlucky way.

At that point, Blooble unmasked himself too, but before Rorwa could continue celebrating, he whispered to her, urgently. "Shhh! Keep your voice down! They're everywhere!"

"Who?" whispered Mark.

"Clover and Velostic's forces!" hissed Nooble.

"Who?" asked Rorwa.

"Some tall, weird super villain who has taken over the city!" said Nooble. "He has captured all the Templarians except us four! Remember Velostic? He was..."

The three were interrupted by Vagar's snoring, "HONK SHOO! HONK SHOO!"

"WAKE UP!" the three screamed. With that, Nooble, Blooble, Rorwa and Mark ran off towards Mark's magic entrance with Vagar following close behind, grumbling. Half–asleep he had barely registered the return of their strange old companions, Nooble and Blooble.

As the trio ventured deeper into the forest towards the secret entrance, they had to stop several times for Mark. The long journey was taking its toll, and he would have much preferred to be in a library with his Templarian–funded crossonte (croissant) and moffrer (coffee), helping to discover new research for different types of steel, or providing tactical support from the HQ with magical ear pieces.

"Are we there yet, I'm hungry," whined Mark as he got a smack round the back of his round head. "Ooow, my head. Why are you so evil?" he snarled, gripping a random rock and throwing it at Vagar.

When they had gone far enough into the forest they found the secret path that Mark had led them to. They turned, and went forwards, back towards the city.

"Are we there yet?" Vagar complained.

"No," Rorwa replied.

"Are we there yet?" Vagar complained again.

"No," Rorwa replied again.

"Are we there yet?" Vagar complained AGAIN.

"No," Rorwa replied AGAIN, "And also I feel deja–vu."

"Are we there yet?" Vagar complained.

"No," Rorwa replied.

"Are we there yet?" Vagar complained again.

"No," Rorwa replied again.

"Are we there yet?" Vagar complained AGAIN.

"Stop," Rorwa stated. "And I still feel deja–vu."

"Can both of you just stop," Mark paused. "Stop, please." They started to see the sun in the treetops, and they started to feel colder.

"Are we there yet?" Vagar asked. Rorwa slapped him across the face with the force of a hammer.

"Fool," said Vagar, rubbing his face in pain. "Now I have one more question for you." A smile spread across his face. "Are we there y–"

Rorwa punched him forcefully in the stomach. Vagar started coughing and tripped down onto the floor of the great forest.

"Deserved," Mark and Rorwa said in unison. They continued forward. When the adventurers finally got to the border, but then Rorwa stopped them. The entrance that Mark had known about stood before them – but it was locked by powerful magic. Mark decided to use his wand to open the door, so they could get to the other side. He tried to say the spell. He tried and tried and tried and TRIED! But to no avail.

"What is wrong, Mark?" asked Rorwa.

"Umm... during my imprisonment by the basilisks, they took away my spell book. And I forgot the correct spell," mumbled Mark.

"You and your spell book! You must remember it!" groaned Rorwa angrily.

"I don't!" cried Mark.

"Let's just go to the border, and turn ourselves in!" interrupted Vagar. Before the other three could stop him, he approached a watch tower, where the guards were on look-out. "Hel-lo!" he yelled to the guards. "My name is Vagar and these are my friends Mark and Rorwa!" Rorwa slapped her head in frustration. Nooble was offended Vagar had forgotten him and Blooble – were they not friends? Not that it seemed to matter: the guards were intent on arresting all of them.

About 20 minutes later, they were on their way to a court somewhere across the border. They had come to realise something terrible had happened to the Templarian city under the new Grandmaster, it was under a terrifying regime. Lykos were patrolling the streets and the borders, the whole city was like a prison.

"Well done, Vagar!" growled Rorwa. "Your way of getting us across the border is stupid, but works, and not in a good way either!" She was not looking forward to being locked up again. Then they crossed a bridge. It was a long way down to the water. Luckily, she could tell that the water was deep, so Rorwa started to wiggle her hands about and freed herself while the guards were snoring. Then she freed Nooble, Blooble, Mark and Vagar and the four jumped into the water. They fell down and away from the truck and into the river. SPLASH! The current dragged them away.

"Let's start getting back to the shore." announced Rorwa.

The news of the prisoners' escape quickly reached the Grandmaster's quarters.

"Masters!" said young Templarian who had burst in. "It's the prisoners!"

"What about them?" snarled Velostic. "Already dead?'

"No, sir," the young Templarian looked meek. "They've escaped!"

At this news, Velostic could feel his insides burn. His bones feel like they were broken, all at once. "I'll see to this," he said, disappearing into the Grandmaster's chambers.

From beyond, Clover sat watching. He had seen his plan fall into place right in front of his eyes. Every little bit was slotting right in. He smiled as he watched the group falling for his trap. Oh, how nice it felt. The old leader was dead, now it was time for Clover's plan to pick away at the Templarian order until it fell apart, like what they had done to him and his family. His eyes changed from a calm ocean blue to a bright glowing red. It was all going to work out after all.

Just then, Velostic felt his mind being searched, and he knew he mustn't resist. His entire life flashed through his mind in a matter of seconds and he reeled backwards with the shock of sudden release.

"Remember, Velostic. Rorwa, Mark, Vagar – they might all prove quite useful." Velostic smiled, as he went to seek them out.

When they had finally reached the shoreline, it didn't take very long for Rorwa, Mark, Nooble, and Vagar to start planning their next move– and it didn't take very much longer than that for them to start bickering about it.

"We should go and attack Velostic," Vagar stated.

"Why?" Rorwa asked.

"He set this up," Vagar responded. "It's his fault y'know,"

"Well..." said Rorwa.

"We attack him, become the leaders and live a happy life," said Vagar, as if this was the conversation ender.

"No," Rorwa countered. "That is not at all feasible."

"Why?" Vagar was confused and questioning, just as Rorwa had been a moment ago.

"Because," Rorwa stared into the river, its water so deep it felt like an abyss, "However lovely that is, it's not at all realistic. First of all, back in the day, Velostic was so much better."

"No, we were better." Vagar was confident this time.

"Well," Rorwa sighed, "You wouldn't remember what happened then."

Vagar just stared at Rorwa.

"Oh never mind." Rorwa laid down on the tent floor. "It wouldn't even work anyway."

"Why?" said Vagar, plaintively. He was getting tired of

arguing.

"The wall, and the entire Templarian army is against us,"

"You know," Blooble chimed in, "I agree with Rorwa here."

Vagar was obstinate: "You can all suffer in our current situation. I'll be retired and relaxing in my boats, plural, when my plan eventually works."

"Still dreaming?" sighed Nooble. "And anyway, how are we going to get in?"

Rorwa twisted up her mouth in disapproval. "I'm telling you, that's impossible. The best chance we have is to try and escape."

The others did not seem convinced by Rorwa's logic. Nooble and Blooble were intent on coming up with their own ideas. "Hmmmmmmmmmmm..." mused Nooble.

"What?" asked Blooble.

"I know!" cried Nooble.

"Yes?!" asked Blooble.

Nooble paused. "No..." he muttered.

"I know! We should get some more people to help us!"

Rorwa considered. "That... Is a good idea! Much better than Vagar's idiotic idea. But who can help us?"

Everyone thought for a while.

"The only people I can remember that were nice to us were James and Arcus," said Nooble eventually.

"Who?" asked Rorwa.

"The two prisoners who helped us escape? Anyway, I want to know what happened to them."

"Probably living in luxury, with stolen money bags all around them..." muttered Vagar.

"Shut up, Vagar. Don't butt in!" growled Mark.

"I'm trying to be realistic," protested Vagar.

Rorwa was getting fed up of the squabbling– they needed a firm plan of action, and fast. "I may not approve of attacking Velostic's forces... but I would rather charge down their throats and go down in a blaze of glory, than sit on my backside!" she cried, wringing her hands desperately. The fact that she had been thrown off the basilisk throne seemed to have knocked her confidence. The dark circles underneath her eyes were visible even in the moonlit night. She stood up and, dragging her legs exhaustedly, walked into the woods.

"Well she seems to be having a tantrum like a child. Now who agrees with me?" Nooble asked as he turned to look at the group.

"No, we are not doing that!" stated Vagar as thunder rolled in the distance. Vagar's eyelids kept flickering down for extended periods, but even in his exhausted state, his grizzled appearance instilled fear in all but the very lucky Blooble.

"Who put you in charge?" cried Mark, as he stood up from the log he was sitting on.

"Yeah," grunted Blooble, stepping forward towards Vagar. He felt that he didn't need to worry, since he had an unnaturally lucky streak going for the entirety of his life, but when he was greeted by a hard set of knuckles to his chin, he reeled back in shock. Electricity flowed through Blooble's body as he fell against a large tree. *Ouch.* That was going to turn into a large bruise.

As Rorwa sat by the lukewarm water of the little river, surrounded by trees, she thought about the options that the rest of the gang had presented to her. Maybe what she had said in frustration was truer than she had realised. They couldn't wait around forever, so perhaps a risky strategy, going down in a blaze of glory, really was better than camping out with Vagar, Mark, Nooble, and Blooble, who were all at each others' throats. There was one way into the city that she knew of, one that she had hesitated to remind the others about. She sighed, and turned on her heel to walk back towards the others, still sitting on the beach. The dragon lair was the best way to sneak into the city, and she had to tell them so.

By the next day, they had successfully made it through the dragon lair, although they had become fairly scorched in the process, and Vagar had an unpleasant slash mark down one arm. From the exit of the lair, it was a quick and easy walk to their destination, the Mage's palace.

"Don't do anything rash," Mark told Rorwa and Vagar once inside the Mage's palace. "We have plenty of time to find those who are against Clover. So keeping a low profile is a lot more important, especially since Velostic has been floating around inspecting anything out of the ordinary, and he has long forgotten us as friends. He'll kill us faster than any of the dragons wanted to."

The group split up, and calmly walked through different corridors in the Mage's palace. Despite all their differences they had one thing in common: all was calm on the surface.

Eventually, Mark, Rorwa, Nooble, and Blooble's paths all met. The only person still scouting around the Mage's Palace alone was Vagar, but he could certainly look after himself. So they continued down the hall and past some suits of armour. One was thin and another was a bit bigger than the rest. Mark felt goosebumps on his skin. Something wasn't right. Nooble heard some clanking behind him. He gulped and turned around. The suits of armour stopped moving. So the gang kept going... and the suits of armour started following them again. Rorwa sighed.

"I'm tired of this. It's getting ridiculous," she said. She knocked the two helmets off the suits of armour and revealed two familiar faces.

"James? Arcus?" cried Nooble astonished. "Oh gosh. Hi Nooble!" cried Arcus, grinning.

"We were going to shoot you and your friends! We thought you were spies or something," said Nooble, aghast.

"Then Arcus spoiled it by talking," muttered James. "Anyway... what's going on?"

"We're going after Velostic," explained Mark. "Remember him?"

"Yes. We're going after him because he's taken over the city," Rorwa chipped in.

"Ok, ok," muttered Arcus. "Do you guys know how much money we're going to make if we get him?" he said quickly. James slapped his head in frustration. Rorwa sighed, Arcus's motivation seemed to be all wrong.

"It doesn't matter whether there's a bounty on Velostic's head, he wants to kill us! Us abandoning the city will only have made the situation worse," Rorwa hoped that Arcus and James would see sense, but they looked unconvinced. "You tell them, Nooble, maybe they'll listen to you." So Nooble explained to his old cell-mates that Velostic was working under the evil Clover, and how important it was to defeat him.

"So, you want to take out Velostic?" said James. The brothers nodded. "Good luck doing that. You'll need it, especially if you're planning to assassinate him alone. Anyway you forget someone who could and would help you."

"And who is that person?" Blooble inquired.

"You really don't remember our time in the prison?" James asked, surprised. "Wow, time really does flow fast for some of us." He half laughed.

Rorwa stared at James, pondering what he meant.

"Stop staring at me like a petrified cat," James chuckled. "Yshkavis... you really don't remember her?"

Vagar chuckled, "Ab–so–lute–ly no way. That is a death wish."

"She would absolutely be down for a raid on Velostic and his brave Templarians," James said, "You would be surprised. Not to mention she commands about 200 prison guards with ravenous lykos. You want her on your side, trust me."

Arcus and James were engaged in a heated debate about whether or not to reveal how much money they were making from the bounty hunting business. Nooble decided to step in, pulling James away while Mark dragged Arcus aside before the dispute could escalate into a fight.

"Ok, so now we can continue our search," said Mark, his voice impatient.

"WAIT!" cried Rorwa. She made everyone jump. "How about we split up? Some of us can go and find Velostic, while the other team goes to persuade Yshkavis to join our rebellion."

The group stopped for a minute and thought about who was going to be in which team.

"So I'll decide," announced Rorwa. "Vagar's team will go to Yshkavis' prison while my team is going to search the palace! And properly, this time. I know none of us have found him so far, but that doesn't mean we give up!"

"Who put you in charge?" yelled Blooble.

"Shut up Blooble," grumbled Mark. "I know! Blooble can go with you."

Mark pushed Blooble towards Rorwa, who sighed.

"Ok," she continued. "Nooble, Blooble, and Arcus can come with me, and Vagar, James and Mark will be with each other. Speaking of Vagar, where is he?"

The group looked around the hallway. They heard some groaning noises and the clanging of metal. Instantly, the warriors dived to hide behind the dark, dusty furniture. Rorwa hid in a cupboard. Sadly for her it was the wrong place to hide, as there was a metal spring inside it that launched her out of the tiny space and smashed her against the wall. Luckily, the impact wasn't fatal. Then a few seconds later, Vagar was flung out of the cupboard as well: it was a secret passage. Vagar moaned as he rubbed his aching back and face.

"Well that's the last time I poke my nose into a drawer." he mumbled. "I fell in and it was a passage, which has flung me all around the place until now."

Rorwa's team continued their hunt around the palace for Velostic. Coming across a creaky, cobwebby door, Rorwa gestured for the others to stay well back– she had a feeling something important or dangerous could be behind the door. Rorwa lifted the latch silently. Her chain–mailed hand grasped around the short sword, stolen from one of the guards she had killed in the fight against Vordik. That felt like a lifetime ago to Rorwa. She shivered even though the temperature of the warm summer night was well above average. Her limbs seemed too heavy to carry. She didn't realise that she had continued on, her instincts driving her, but she found herself at the bottom of a raven house, many stories tall.

As she turned to go, a force sent her flying down the 20 metre tower. She cried out, and even as she fell her head was turning wildly trying to find her attacker. Then she felt its whiskers brush up against her face: it was a leopardi, a big cat with a rare talent for invisibility, that had knocked her down the tower, and it had pounced after her to attack her some more. She felt her back collide with the cold stone floor. She vaulted herself up, summoning her weapon to her hand, and she challenged the beast. It was an impressive four metres long, the biggest animal she had ever seen.

Her accomplices, who had been waiting for her to return, jumped back in surprise. The first to recover was Arcus, and he launched himself forwards to attack the leopardi…

It was no easy feat to defeat the feline beast, but working together they skillfully overcame it, and soon it lay in a furry heap at the base of the tower. Perhaps it was partly down to Blooble's lucky streak. Either way, the group was determined not to let anything, man or beast, get in their way.

Chapter 14

Seeking out Yshkavis

Mark, James, and Vagar had been trekking away from the Mage's Palace for about 2 hours on their own quest to find Yshkavis. Mark's pathfinder – a softly glowing ball of air – provided them with a clear view of the twig–strewn winding forest path.

"Mark, is this safe?" Vagar asked "This light would demonstrate our presence to anyone who cares within 500 metres."

Mark signed and they were plunged into total darkness. Mark had known the risk, but he also realised that time was of the essence – the light would show them the fastest route to their destination, the prison of Haster.

"The fastest way isn't always the safest way. Follow my voice, I'm the only one who can sense the pathfinder. Unless you want to stay for the night?" That was directed at Vagar who grunted and pushed on uphill. Just as they reached the summit of halfway–hill (as Mark had sarcastically named it), a downpour began, which beat the pathfinder to the ground and drenched them within seconds. Vagar signed disappointedly and motioned to James that perhaps staying the night really was the only option. Even after they were in their cloth tent with the waterproof coating Mark had put on it, Vagar had an uneasy feeling that they hadn't killed the light early enough to avoid unwanted notice.

Vagar yawned as he walked out of the tent, playfully smacking James on the head when he made his exit. As he pulled the magic tent–peg, the magic tent disappeared, along with its smell of rich incense and its infinite food. God knew how Mark had found it in the Basilisks' lair. The others grunted as their comfortable beds were removed.

"Morning," cried Vagar as he grabbed a water skin from his belt. "Let's get going."

Suddenly, James caught sight of something towering behind

Vagar. "Curse you, you Valyrian," hissed James as he grabbed a dagger and threw it at the giant man. The rest of the group narrowed their eyes in confusion– was James calling Vagar a name? What even was a Valyrian?

"What is a Valyrian?" asked Mark, saying out loud what everyone else was thinking, as he calmly dug out some bread to eat.

"We are Valyrians," boomed a low voice. The rest of the company whipped around to find a group of five men dressed in chain–mail and large pieces of armour. Mark, in all his magical knowledge was completely lost– in fact, only James seemed to know what was going on.

"Oooh sweet mail of Zod. We are in deep trouble," said James as he drew his long hunting knife.

An axe came whistling through the air towards Vagar. Luckily, he ducked down in the nick of time, and it lodged in a tree.

"Well done Zerlock," snorted Vagar at Mark as he picked up the massive axe. He muttered a few words of prayer directed to his great grandfathers who had merged the Templarian and Valyrian civilizations together letting them dominate the other factions.

The tallest of the Valyrians overheard Vagar's muttered words and, to the company's shock, gave a low bow, eventually raising his head to look expectantly at Vagar. Vagar felt anxious, but his tough, grizzled face would never show nerves outwardly– he tried to play it cool. For once, he didn't have to depend on his powers– the Valyrians would be far more useful as allies, just as they had once been allied to his ancestors, than as enemies who had to be electrified.

James still looked a little distrustful, but Mark raised his eyebrows, impressed. They were gathering more and more powerful beings on their side, and perhaps that would give them the edge in confronting Clover and Velostic.

Clearly, Vagar was thinking the same thing. "Valyrians! Recruit more of your ranks, send them to us in peace, and we will reward you." One Valyrian gave a curt nod, and the group set off back into the forest.

"Interesting," remarked Clover, watching the confrontation between the Templarians and the Valyrians through the Crystal

Orb. Velostic was perched at Clover's right–hand side, looking down on the group with the strange Mercenaries, seeming a little confused. The overlord answered his servant's question before it was even asked, "Valyrian Mercenaries, a rebellious group of mages who played a role in the battle of Corviaskh." Clover stepped up from his chair, searching through the seemingly infinite bookshelves. "Ah, here." Clover grabbed a book with a greyish green cover from the bookshelf containing battle records. "The battle of Corviaskh, one of the most contested points during the Templarian War." Clover flicked through the pages quickly. "Page 219, Chapter 15, Paragraph 5 line 5." He smiled, reading on "The war was won by no–one, lost by all."

"Ok, we're here," sighed Vagar, marching up to the gates of the ice prison. The view was very different compared to the last time they'd set eyes on it all those months ago. It was the hottest summer since 345 AD.

James and Mark were gasping and were desperate for water. It was about 60 degrees Celsius and it was probably hotter than the Ralpmet desert east of Templarian City. This place was meant to be the coldest place on the earth!

"O...K..." gasped Mark.

"Why are we here in the first place?" mumbled James, his lips were dry and he was desperately fumbling for his water bottle.

"So we can get Yshkavis on our side, remember?" cried Vagar.

"OK, OK. How are we gonna get inside?" asked Mark.

"How should I know, Mark?" asked Vagar. "After all, you're the braaaaaiiinnns!"

Mark scoffed and walked to the gates. On either side of the doors, the guards were snoring. He didn't know why: they were the night guards and it was 2:00 in the morning. Mark took out a bottle with some powder in it and a matchbox. He opened the bottle and inserted the powder into the keyhole. Then he struck a match and lit the keyhole. In a few seconds, the lock was broken and the gate was opened. The trio walked inside and there were guards sleeping all around them. James and Vagar crept quietly behind the wizard and past the guards. It was like some spell had descended upon them. James was avoiding the guards ever so carefully, while Vagar attempted to fly again. It had been a long time since he'd flown. Then he kicked a sleeping guard by accident and awoke him.

"Snork! Huh?" The guard jumped up and yelled: "HEY! INTRUDERS!" The other guards jumped up and surrounded the three. Mark opened his bag quickly and took out a bunch of bottles, but then a guard hit him with a spear and, in shock, Mark dropped all except one of them back into his bag. A bottle containing a black potion hit the ground and broke at the feet of a menacing looking guard.

A glittering black confusion cloud floated out of the bottle like steam. It hovered around the guard's face, and spread out towards the other three henchmen, who started to look a little muddled. Although it was working so far, Vagar side-eyed the cloud nervously, not sure if such a flimsy looking thing could keep the guards from noticing the break-in. He kicked in the decorative door and walked into Ysh's office. She appeared to be out. Mark dispelled the cloud and fixed the door with one smooth motion of his arm. The guards hadn't noticed anything.

"We wait for her here," James announced and they made themselves comfortable on an expensive imported leather sofa designed to intimidate visitors with a display of wealth.

Sitting on the couch. Vagar suddenly thought of something that could backfire and spoil their plans!

"What would happen if Yshkavis doesn't want to join?" Vagar gulped. "What if it completely backfires and we all end up in jail and there wouldn't be any of us to come and rescue the Templarians? What happen if Yshkavis sends us to jail?" Vagar started chewing his nails nervously. He walked around the place. "What happens if she doesn't accept? Oh dear oh dear oh dear oh dearrrr..." They waited for an hour for Yshkavis to come but she didn't turn up. By then, Vagar's blood had started to turn cold. He started to freeze up, turning to a block of ice on the chair. His teeth started to chatter.

"Calm down, Vagar!" sighed James. "You don't need to worry!"

"W-w-w-why d-d-o-on't I h-h-have t-t-t-oo w-w-worry about Ysh-Ysh-Ysh-Yshkavis?-?-?" asked Vagar, his teeth still chattering.

"Because, she bears a lot of grudges against Velostic," answered James. "I knew her almost 10 years ago at the academy."

"What academy?" asked Mark. James took out a couple of

scarves out of his bag and wrapped them around Vagar before he literally turned into a block of ice. Then, he began his story.

The academy had been a strange time of Velostic's life–and James painted such a realistic picture of it, that the gang almost believed they were watching his younger years. There was Velostic, sitting in the mess hall. He gripped his knife as the resident bullies, Clooble and his gang of thugs, poked fun at Velostic. Suddenly, Velostic used one hand to fling the knife into the table, and with the other hand, grasped Clooble by the throat and lifted him up. The retching sound coming out of Clooble's throat made him sick. In a split second, Clooble was dropped onto the table. Velostic used magic to levitate the knife and was about to plunge it into Clooble's throat…

But a white light stopped the blade in its path. Yshkavis stood in the academy hallway, her eyes glowing bright.

"Bloody hell, cousin! I told you not to kill him." she cried, as she dashed forward and smacked the testosterone filled teen.

At that moment, Vagar interrupted James's story, pulling the gang out of the vision. "Wait a minute, Velostic was Yshkavis's cousin? I knew that all the old Templarian families were interconnected. But I never knew that."

"Velostic and Ysh were cousins and both of them were after top roles in the TDCMO. But Velostic got there first. He said that he did it because it changes people. And it does. Last time I saw him he looked broken. His eyes were different… like he was ready to kill me in a millisecond, which I don't doubt he could have. He was colder. He used to love to hang out with the boys and do all those teenage things... but now he's evil. He's spoken about having to kill too many people, having to do things he couldn't tell me."

Vagar considered James's account. "Yeah, I heard about that, they say that although it is one of the best paid jobs in the order and gets your family noble rank, there's a dark side to the TDCMO."

"Any leverage we can use to turn Ysh against Velostic?" asked Mark, hoping that the other two would get to the point a little faster.

"Don't think so, unless..." James sat up straight from where he had been slouched on the leather sofa and continued with his vivid story.

A crowd of students in a cavernous hall, Velostic and Yshkavis among them, stared up at two imposing instructors. "Welcome, to the TDCMO," bellowed the first, "Only some of you will be here at the end of this assessment."

"This test is split into ten different sections," said the second instructor, "Two of which will be today,"

"The first section, is the written section," shouted the first instructor, "and it will last three hours." The first instructor death-stared one of the students, "And there will be 250 questions, totalling 500 marks."

"The passing mark will be anything over 450 marks, or 90%." The second instructor shouted, "We are your instructors, Allan and Makein."

The 300 students went through the questions with caution, except Yshkavis and Velostic. And sooner than later, the three hours were up.

"Please hand in your papers," Allan boomed.

Once every paper was handed off to the marker, the second section was announced.

"The second section is Magical Theory." Makein bellowed, before a loud groan was heard from the students. "It is 2 hours long."

And like the first tests, they zoomed through it, and the day was over. Then they zoomed through day 2, the tests being Magical History and Magic Uses in Ancient Times. And day 3, the tests being The Elemental Base of Magic and The Science of Magic. They even zoomed through day 4, commonly known as the sludge, with the tests being Magic Deconstruction and Magical Theory, plus the most enjoyable test of the day, Runic Construction and Rune meanings.

Finally came day 5, when the final test was held. This was Magic Application, known by students as 'Hell incarnate,' 'Harder than the sun is warm' and other colourful names, because, well, IT WAS REALLY REALLY HARD. The test itself was split into three parts: combat dexterity, magic construction, and the third part, where Yshkavis' life was changed, and where a flaming crimson rage was born.

Velostic finished off the charm which should cure the human sitting opposite of him of blindness. The patient opened one eye.

"Half cured," the inspector announced. Velostic was still one of the best, tied point to point to Yshkavis, since they had the same score in combat dexterity and construction. Only the best would be taken into the spec ops division. He began to prepare a ball of magic, keeping it secret from the inspector who was admiring the way Ysh was handling her patient. The ball of magic struck the patient, shielding him from Yshkavis's charm. Ysh frowned at the human who had stopped being susceptible to her magic. The instructor frowned, and wrote something on a pad of paper.

When the scores were announced, Velostic and Yshkavis were in the top three for almost all of the tests, except for Magic Application. Allan's voice had been booming over a loudspeaker for 20 minutes already, and Velostic was starting to daydream. However, he tuned back in when he heard Allan wrapping up.

"But for the first time in years," Allan was saying, "a member of the top three did not pass, that member being Yshkavis, due to their low score in the final test." Yshkavis's mouth hung open in shock. But Velostic was smiling, as they read out his own name: he was finally going to be a spec ops member.

That was where James finished his story.

"This is great!" Vagar announced "Not Velostic cheating. But now we've got some leverage – a chance to get Ysh. When she hears the plan she'll be as good as on our side!"

"Ok, you two," interrupted Mark. "But how can we be sure?"

"I just told you," said James, impatiently "she has a grudge against Velostic because he cheated in the last test all those years ago, y'know, in the academy..."

"It's very simple!" began Vagar in the manner of a teacher lecturing a slow student. "We'll just present the evidence: 'Velostic is out to abuse his position as Grandmaster of the Templarians. Yshkavis will think for a moment, and then join us in the rebellion. Then we defeat Velostic..', problem solved!"

Vagar seemed triumphant, as if he had won the argument by presenting this simple series of facts.

"Just one moment..." piped up Mark. "There's a problem... What if Yshkavis thinks that is a stupid idea and throws us all in prison?"

James hesitated for a moment. "I didn't think of that..."

The three of them slumped into the leather sofa, feeling

deflated. Mark was reading a pocket book about how to mentally break someone's mind. James was sat looking off into space remembering the good old days back at the academy. Vagar was sharpening his daggers. They stayed here for quite some time, until…

"Wait! I have a better idea," said James.

"What do you mean?" asked Vagar.

"My idea will probably get her on our side without the risk of us getting chucked into the hellhole they call a prison!" announced James triumphantly.

"What is it?" they demanded.

"You'll have to wait and see…" James told them smugly.

As James said this, the group froze, hearing the unmistakable scrap, scrap, scrap of Lyko claws.

"Ambush," whispered Vagar, as he moved to hide behind the door. The others couldn't respond as the large wolf–like thing entered the room– only to have its throat slit by Vagar and its dead body shoved into a tall cupboard.

"Wait! There's something tied around its neck," said Mark as he knelt down.

"It's a letter," said James as he knelt down to open it. "With Velostic's personal seal," he began to read its contents out loud. "Dear Cousin, I thank you so much for supporting my claim to the title of Grandmaster. I have therefore put you forward for a promotion as head of the TDCMO. I know that it is your dream job. If there is anything I can do to help you on your travels to the capital, just say the word. Velostic. P.S. I have given you your favourite office, the one looking out on the city. I know, I am great."

"That has just given me an idea," said Mark as he scrambled for paper and ink.

"Really? Are you sure?" Vagar grabbed Mark's hand, trying to stop him.

"Well, do you have a better way? Trust me," said Mark with a dark tone coming into his voice.

Once Mark had re–drafted the letter, the gang left Yshkavis's reception room and waited in the shadowy corridor until they spotted her entering the office at long last. Since she left the door ajar, they watched her as she sat down, starting her work for the day by looking at reports. She pulled out a file with the title, Prisoner 677–E.

"Recent incidents," she said scanning through the document. "None, that's a surprise." But she couldn't finish the file, as there was a knock on the door. "Come in," Ysh shouted, spinning round to face the door.

"There is a letter for you." Her mailman handed her a letter. Then James approached the mailman from behind, tapping him on the shoulder with a beseeching look, "And a guest," added the mailman. Mark smiled appreciatively.

"Send him in," she said, and Mark stepped smoothly into the office.

"Hello, this letter is of Great Importance to the Templarian leader, Velostic." James said, "Thou must comply."

"Let's see." She opened the letter,

The letter read:

Due to recent changes in the Templarian Royalty, there have been a list of 5 Major Changes, with 15–20 more in the Voting and Editing Process. There is also a list of changes to your prison.
1. No keeping leopardi or lykos as personal pets.
2. No heating during winter months to conserve energy.
3. Reduced income to higher ranking members of society to reduce poverty.
4. The Grandmaster has the power to veto any existing law or code.

Here are the changes to your prison.
1. Increased physical workouts to head prison staff.
2. New filing system, (Block – Prisoner Number – Crime ID)
3. New Crime ID System, Each crime has a unique 5 letter long text id. E.g. Shoplifting is S#/..
4. No personal items in an official office.
5. All paperwork must be revised and redone quarterly.
6. You have to send lots of birthday presents to family members, especially your favourite cousin.

As she read through the long list of rules, Ysh's face got redder and redder.

"Who does Velostic think he is?" she exclaimed, her fingers trembling. "He's the Supreme leader and Grandmaster of the Templarians," answered James meekly.

"I got that..." muttered Yshkavis, "But how did he come into power?"

"He bribed, hired, and made his followers rig the votes by threatening them."

"Why didn't anyone stand up to him?"

"I just told you, Yshkavis, they were threatened with exile or imprisonment. They're too afraid to do anything."

"Afraid? Why?"

"I wish someone would stand up to him, someone like, I don't know... like you?"

"I'll think about joining," said Yshkavis. "If Velostic does anything worse, I'll definitely join, OK?" James nodded.

At some point in the conversation, the mailman had departed quietly. Clearly he had been instructed to enforce the new rules, because he had taken her Lyko with him. She laughed: that would not go well. He was a biter. Taking her pet was a low blow from Velostic– perhaps she really should join forces with this James person.

"Get out," she addressed James, "I have some–" but she was cut short as a mass of random people entered her office without knocking. Yshkavis stared at them indignantly. One of them was carrying a bucket.

"What are you doing?" she shouted at the men sticking up posters. The hammers and nails rattled in her astounded ears.

"Ma'am, we are just doing our jobs." The workers said calmly. "This is not my choice."

She stared at the posters, and one look made her bang her head against the wall.

"What of GOD are those?" She half-shouted and half-laughed, realising that it was Velostic's face on the posters. "Let me have a look!"

She burst out laughing even more.

"B–belie–believe y–your leader," Ysh laughed. "D–dont questi–" She bent over in stitches. "Life is short, Make it worth it, Support Velostic? Did he use a super–unadvanced text engine, or some artificial unintelligence to make these?"

The workers continued banging the poster frames into the wall. "Are you questioning Velostic? Unfortunately he's our leader."

"And my cousin," she sighed. "For the love of the Holy

Templarians, I will not have this insolent fool on the throne! I will have my cousin's head!" she screamed, releasing a blast of magic energy which knocked down the guards removing her belongings.

"Very well, Commander," said James as he bowed and retreated out of the room. As he walked back into the hall, leaving Ysh to her own devices, he wiped the sweat from his seemingly permanently creased forehead.

Mark had a plan. He slipped out of the shadows of the chambers and pulled the posters off the wall, one by one placing each on the stones in front of his feet. He only needed one of each kind, but he couldn't risk being noticed by the Commander's guards. Through casting a silent sympathetic bond over each poster, he transformed 'BELIEVE YOUR LEADER' to 'DON'T BELIEVE YOUR LEADER, HE IS BEHIND SCAM CALLS!'. Next up was 'DON'T QUESTION, JUST FOLLOW' which had now become inverted: 'JUST QUESTION, DON'T FOLLOW!'

He took a step back from the two posters he had transformed so far, smirking to himself at his success. "Not bad," he remarked under his breath.

The third poster was a classic campaign slogan: 'LIFE IS SHORT, MAKE IT WORTH IT! SUPPORT VELOSTIC'. Mark chuckled, murmuring "As if!" He cast the sympathetic bond once again; the text now read, "LIFE IS SHORT, IF YOU OBEY VELOSTIC IT WILL BE SHORTER".

At that moment, Mark was startled by footsteps behind him: it was Ysh. He turned to face her, eyes widened with fear.

The two stood in silence for what seemed like years before Ysh finally spoke.

"I will help your cause. This will be my revenge."

They both turned back to the array of posters Mark had left on the floor. Ysh smiled in satisfaction, pointing at the final poster to be transformed.

"What are you going to do about that one?"

The final poster read, 'ARE YOU QUESTIONING VELOSTIC?' with a menacing image accompanying it.

"Easy," Mark replied. One last bond and he had removed the image, replacing it with a line of text so that the poster now read, 'ARE YOU QUESTIONING VELOSTIC? YES? GOOD FOR YOU'.

Chapter 15

The Castle Defences

Penetrating the defences of the Templar City was not going to be easy.

On tall stony turrets all around the castle, there were huge ballistas which could smash even the largest of structures on sight: they had a heavy steel tipped bolt that would explode on impact, burning and knocking down any survivors. Some of the ballistas on floating outposts around the fortress had been adapted to fire a hail of small arrows rather than a large bolt which would rain death upon the enemy. The golems that were manning the ballistas were tireless and had an almost unlimited supply of arrows, enough to destroy several million soldiers with some left over.

"That's not even all of it," Rorwa sighed, looking at the battlements stretching as high as the nearby mountains. "Look at those walls. Why so many cannons?"

"Over 200 cannons in just the South Western Patrol district," James said matter-of-factly, reading from a scroll he had swiped from Ysh's office, "Not to mention those sniper towers."

"Fire cannons, effectively." Mark sighed, "Speed of lightning, damage of a sniper."

"Not to forget the fact that–" James stared on in shock as an explosion the size of the walls was triggered. "Yeah, we need to think again...It looks like you have to get past the standing Garrison of 120,000 soldiers with a force of a thousand leopardi." At their puzzled looks he added, "They're a species of massive leopards, all of which have been bound to the Grandmaster's will. Which is slightly terrifying."

Rorwa held tightly onto her knife. A presence was patrolling the walls; her senses were flooded by it. She watched as Vagar cowered next to her, his new axe strapped onto his back.

He had real fear in his eyes – she had never seen an emotion like that in him. They had fought for years, but this was new to her. She looked at the stolen blueprints for the city. The barracks had doubled in size. The massive intelligence department was made larger. Massive automatons patrolled the buildings and, of course, the parliamentary chambers had been made more lavish. All the more reason to overthrow Velostic's regime.

She sighed. "Right, let's get on with it."

Rorwa led the way to a bridge crossing the moat of the castle, which contained the next line of defence according to James' scroll: Fire sharks.

"Oh...this is not my day, is it?" Rorwa lamented. "Sharks are a common defence, but FIRE sharks? That's a bit cheesy, isn't it?"

"Let's just get through," sighed Nooble. He crossed the bridge and, right then, a shark fired at him. "YIKES!" He cried, jumping and running back to the other side.

"How do we get past them?" asked Arcus.

"I have an idea..." thought Blooble, disappearing into the forest. About 20 minutes later, he came back with a big sack...of ice! "Ice? Where did you get ICE from?" asked Rorwa.

"None of your concern," Blooble smirked, "I have my ways."

"What is that for?"

"You'll see," smiled Blooble.

He stood over the bridge and dumped the entire sack in the water. The sharks swam away quickly, repelled by the freezing cold ice.

"Problem solved!" laughed Blooble. "Let's go."

The gang burst into cheers and took turns patting Blooble on the back, until Rorwa cleared her throat and said, "Come on guys, we've got more to do."

Rorwa led the group over the bridge and through a narrow passageway carved into the castle, lined with high stone walls. Gazing up, she could see devilish ghosts peering down at her from all sides. All she could hear was the deafening silence emitted by the creatures. They crept through the passage, one by one, trying their best to avoid detection.

After what felt like hours of sneaking through the narrow passage, the walls opened up onto a cavern, so tall that Rorwa couldn't even see the ceiling. All she could see was a flying wooden ship emitting a purple glow, patrolling the clearing, full of mages in black cloaks that were endlessly casting spells.

"Wait here, I've got an idea!" yelled Rorwa over the loud

screeches of the mages.

"What's she doing?" demanded Blooble. When Rorwa came back she was carrying a large dirty white sheet, the size of three tablecloths.

"Huh?" mumbled Blooble.

"I spotted it on our way in – must be an old tapestry or something."

All of a sudden, she flung the large cloth over the flying ship. The mages started squirming as their spells started to go wrong, shooting and ricocheting off the walls of the cavern.

"Hah!" yelled Rorwa victoriously. Whilst they were distracted, she snuck her team past them.

She found herself in a sombre room full of armour that clanked loudly every time you touched it. The room had all the best weapons: freshly sharpened swords and spiked maces, tremendous bows, and satchels filled with armour piercing arrows.

"Quick, hide!" exclaimed Rorwa. Her, Blooble, and Nooble ducked behind the door. In that second, the arrows began firing out of the satchels in all directions and bouncing off the walls like lasers.

"Oh no," mumbled Blooble with a panicked look on his face.

"This means they know we're here..." Rorwa muttered, "They've sent the mages to look for us."

"Wait, where's Vagar?" said Nooble, realising he hadn't joined the others behind the door.

"Here!" Vagar shouted, peering out from a hollowed out cavern on the other side of the room. "I found a bunch of weapons we can use against the mages."

Before they knew it, the rebels were left to defend themselves against the mages that emerged into the room, seemingly out of nowhere. Vagar tossed the weapons he had discovered to his friends, and they used every ounce of their skill to fight off the vengeful mages.

Shortly, Rorwa sneaked out of the battle and hid behind a wardrobe in the corner of the room which backed onto a tiny barred window. Her plan was to send a message to the Basilisks, in the hopes that the nobles who had opposed her had been subdued. She wrote a message on a tiny scrap of paper in her notebook, addressed to Arda back in Basilisks County.

Bingo! She spotted a raven flying over to its nest on a windowsill opposite, and cooed it over.

She tied the piece of paper to its leg through the bars, and whispered to the raven, "Please take this to Arda." She let it go and watched it gliding away from the castle, wings flapping in the wind.

Meanwhile, Nooble decided to give the last intruder a flying kick. It was a strong kick – he was learning from his peers on this mission. Unfortunately, he missed and hit the wall. He dropped his sword onto the laughing guard's feet. He screamed in pain and clutched his toes. Arcus knocked out the guard with a bat, then did the same to Nooble. He bent down beside him, and hovered his ear above Nooble's mouth to check he was alright.

"Well, at least he's alive," grinned Arcus, "Let's get out of here!" With that, the team ran out of the room, Nooble limp in Arcus' arms. In the frenzy, nobody had realised their good friend, Vagar, had disappeared.

Chapter 16

Finding a Way

Back in the prison office, Yshkavis and her Lyko Ikari were dozing together as they always did.

"Ikari, I have a mission for you." Yshkavis told the Lyko, gently stroking his fur as he rested his head on her lap. Ikari's fur pricked up; he was not used to missions, as he had been a domestic lap pet for many years now.

"We need to send you to gather your friends." She stated, "It seems we will need some assistance..."

Ikari nodded, jumping off Yshkavis' lap and stretching.

And off Ikari went to his homeland.

After what felt like a day of traversing the landscape, he was home in the depths of the Great Jungle.

"Ikari!" His mum shouted.

"Hello, ma'am." Ikari responded. "There is a problem from my land."

"Oh dearie, what?" His mum asked.

"My friend Ysh, the human who saved me..." he trailed off, remembering his mother's hatred of Ysh.

"Yes, I remember her," she snarled. "She took you away from us."

"No, she saved me," Ikari retorted, " Anyway, she needs our help."

"Why?"

"Because this man, Velostic, wants to kill all us Lykos," he lied, "And we need Ysh to help us take out Velostic and keep us safe."

"Darling, of course I'll help you. You know we would always be by your side. I shall command the legion to assist you."

"Thanks, Mum."

Soon enough, the 6th Infantry Regiment of Lykonian Claims was with them, and Ikari led the pack to the City of Templarians.

Vagar awoke in the cavern carved into the side of the armour room, where he had previously retrieved the enchanted weapons. He looked up eagerly as the door opened.

Back during the battle, Rorwa had promised to send someone who could lead him into the city without alerting every guard to his existence, and allow them to launch a more secretive attack on Velostic. The man looked promising, if a bit worn out and scuffed. As Vagar rose to approach him and clap him on the back, he was hit by a flash of recognition.

"Michael?" he gasped. "Hang on...weren't you the guy who was worshiping aardvarks back when we bust out of Yshkavis's prison?"

In that fleeting moment, Vagar's thoughts collided with a mix of curiosity and suspicion. How could he have missed the fact that Michael was on their side all along? Was he an undercover agent? As the gravity of the situation sank in, a surge of questions filled Vagar's head. Had Michael been working covertly for the resistance all this time? Or was there something more intricate at play?

Vagar's gaze fixed on Michael, searching for any signs of deception. The room grew more tense as the realisation settled. Vagar eyed him with a growing mix of disbelief and perhaps newfound respect.

"I'm an undercover agent. I'm here to help you bust into the fortress; you and your girlfriend Rorwa."

"Rorwa's...not my girlfriend," stuttered Vagar, still in shock that this madman was the person who was going to lead him to Clover. He sat down, slightly more dramatically than he had intended, and Michael sat down opposite him to talk strategy. As the man rambled on however, Vagar soon came to realise this plan was just another of his senseless obsessions. He thought he saw a carrot sticking out of Michael's pocket. Nonetheless he decided to see where the madman led him, given he was out of clues himself.

Michael grasped Vagar by the back of his jacket and dragged him out of the castle.

Meanwhile, Mark and Ysh crept up to the gates of the Templarian City and paid the standardised 'privacy fare' used by vagabonds to enter the walls; this was essentially a spell which triggered the guards to have a sudden memory lapse and forget that they were meant to check under travellers' hoods.

"You never saw us..." Mark began.

"And we have no idea who you are," finished the guard – this was the traditional joke phrase which the city's black market would use in shady dealings. Mark unfurled the scroll the other team had sent them. "Now we just follow the map!" he announced, showing the scroll to Ysh.

The others – Rorwa, Arcus, Nooble and Blooble – suddenly burst from a first floor window of the castle, flames roaring behind them.

"You guys okay? What on earth happened in there?" Mark quizzed them, scanning each rebel for any sign of injury. Surprisingly, none.

"Unimportant. Let's go," and at that, Rorwa began storming into the forest.

At the same moment, Michael appeared, dragging Vagar at an almost inhuman speed into the forest. The others caught sight of the pair, merely a blur to them, only identifiable by Vagar yelling "GUYS, COME WITH US!" as they passed. The rest of the rebels sprang into action and followed them.

The magic axe which Vagar held in his hand fell as he was pulled along at an almost inhuman speed. Vagar's thoughts were split between wondering how his battle companion was now one of the best levitating magicians in the world, and how the once insane Michael was suddenly sane. Although, on second thought, he wasn't so sure.

Yshkavis magically appeared beside them, running at the same pace, her hand scooping down to grab the weapon from the floor. "That's better," she muttered. Although she was a compromised prison governor, she was also a Templarian Noble: they had spent their lives training for combat. She was ready.

Somehow, Vagar and Ysh convinced Michael to slow down. "These are our friends, Michael. We need their help. This has to be a team effort."

Chapter 17

Old Enemies and New Allies

As the group of battle-worn rebels wandered through the forest, led by the two veterans, Rorwa was muttering and moving around animatedly. Suddenly, Vagar pulled his new axe from his back.

"Look at this thing – could swipe through a basilisk like no one's business," he growled, running over the blade with his fingers.

"Pathetic," snarled Rorwa, drawing her own sword from its sheath.

"It's not pathetic," he retorted, lifting the weapon in front of him.

"Yes it is!" snarled Rorwa, raising her own weapon.

"Is this how they always behave?" asked James, glancing towards Mark with his eyebrows raised.

"Yep," said Mark as he sat down onto a tree trunk, "Any situation you'd think would be a good time to be serious, they start fighting." he sighed, perching his stubbly chin onto his hands.

The clanging of weapons cut the two's conversation off as Rorwa was blown across the clearing. The axe in Vagar's grasp was now glowing purple and its surface had developed a golden tinge.

"Holy!" screamed Mark and James as they rushed over to the weapon.

"Thanks for the help, guys!" Rorwa's voice called sarcastically from across the clearing.

Ignoring her, James muttered, "This weapon must be made out of Pumararian."

"That would mean that it could kill magical beings, right?" responded Mark as he ran the back of his hand over the weapon. Yshkavis emerged from where she had been waiting in the shadows since the fight erupted.

"Wait! I just remembered something the guards told me. Velostic was supposed to have been executed at the Basilisk lair. How is he still alive?"

"And you only just thought of telling us this?" screamed Rorwa as she rejoined the group.

"That must mean that he was brought back from death at the point between life and death," said James as he stumbled back in shock. For a second he was suspended in a state between disgust and anger, before the reality of their situation dawned on him and he became flooded with fear.

"So Velostic is a ghoul and pretty much immortal. This magical axe might help us," Vagar said.

The rebels found themselves on a huge rocky plain, furnished with jagged boulders which led to steep drops on all sides. The Templar City was built into this unlikely, seemingly hostile environment. The rebellion that they had helped stoke up had rapidly grown in size, and Velostic and his army were engaged in a heated battle against a throng of discontented subjects.

"Ok, we won't have long!" Michael growled as he watched Velostic on the battlefield; him and his leopardi were massacring dozens of men by the second.

"It's fine, I don't need much time," Vagar grunted as he scaled the rock, and hid behind a boulder to watch Velostic's next move.

Michael's eyes were growing beady and urgent; he began retreating from the battlefield.

"I must leave you," he muttered distractedly, as he faded into the distance.

In a split second, Vagar saw Velostic leap down the rocks by the side of the battlefield and disappear from view.

"Here goes nothing," he heard Yshkavis mutter as she leapt onto a rooftop of a house beyond the edge of the plain. Vagar followed. It was a miracle the duo weren't seen as they traversed the rooftops carved into the rock. Once they finally found an open window, the one Velostic must have entered through, they took a peek behind them to make sure no one was following. No guards or leopardi in sight.

However as Vagar and Yshkavis continued on, creeping through dark passageways and surveying the outskirts of the Templar settlement, Velostic was nowhere to be found. It was as if he had disappeared into thin air.

To make matters worse for the rest of the gang, a dust cloud appeared on the horizon, announcing the arrival of another army.

"There are too many of them," cried Nooble in a panic, ducking low behind the rapidly disintegrating parapet.

A laser beam hit the stone, sending splinters flying in all directions.

"Quick! Duck!" yelled Nooble, who just missed one that flew right next to his head. "Phew, that was close," he said with a relieved look on his face.

"Stop trying to escape. It's completely useless!" yelled Velostic fiercely. As soon as he said that, they began sprinting as fast as they could but it was hopeless. They were trapped in a terrible situation. Just as they thought it couldn't get worse, it did. They caught sight of the giant unavoidable cloud of dust caused by Velostic's army, who only cared about protecting their leader. Nooble and the others all started coughing and choking from the swirl of dust and dirt.

"We will keep fighting no matter what, Velostic!" yelled Nooble in anger.

"There's no point! You may as well just give up," cried Velostic with an evil smirk on his demonic face.

"We will keep going," yelled Nooble, "Under any circumstance!"

Rorwa coughed and spluttered and peered through the dust cloud. Everyone was choking. Bloole was hallucinating, and Arcus had run off.

"G–g–g–goodbye Rorwa," shivered Mark. "It was nice knowing you..."

"You too. It's been a pleasure, Mark," admitted Rorwa.

"There's no way we can take them on," whispered Nooble. "I know I have bad luck, but this is bad for all of us!"

Arcus was running around trying to find a way to escape. James held up his arms.

"We surren–"

But before he could finish his sentence, the cloud began to clear.

Rorwa grabbed her sword and was ready to leap at the army. But who was it? Nooble and Mark looked on and gasped. The

Basilisks! Worse than any army in the world!

Blooble fainted.

"OK," gulped Rorwa. In her exhaustion and fear she had momentarily forgotten her summoning of the snakes to their aid. She had been the last Empress Of The Basilisks after all! They were probably after her because she escaped! She gulped and shivered.

Two armies surrounding the rebels: it was either a quick death in battle, or captured and tortured. Rorwa would have chosen the first option.

But then something strange happened. The two great armies yelled and ran and slithered at *each other*. Unbelievably, instead of the Basilisks going after the rebels, they went straight at Velostic's guard and started fighting.

Mark gasped. Arcus had dragged the unconscious Blooble to where everyone was standing. "What's going on?" he mumbled, out of breath, and quickly fainted next to Blooble.

"I don't think fainting is very helpful right now," grumbled Nooble, silently proud of his bravery in staying conscious.

Chapter 18

The Final Showdown

The two sides clashed while the rebels hid, sheltered by a particularly large rock.

"Why are the basilisks helping us?" asked James. "I thought they were your enemies!"

"It was a crazy plan – I don't know how it's worked…maybe they're still loyal to me? I was their Empress once, after all. Or maybe Arda has ordered them here?" cried Rorwa, sheltering from the erupting fight.

With a rumble, a glideship emerged from the clouds above them. It flew low over their heads, and majestically skimmed earthwards. Horrified eyes looked skyward as some began to recognise the ship, decked out with weapons from Velostic's armoury, and capable of launching deadly hamsta–grenades. Finally coming within range, it zoomed past the battlefield, dropping a package into the middle of the basilisk's wooden outpost.

"HAMSTA!" yelled the basilisk leader, and his soldiers leapt for cover as the hamsta exploded, blowing the top of the wooden tower and shredding most of the basilisk soldiers who had been manning the ballista. A gruesome rain of snake–scales rained over the battlefield. The destruction exposed basilisks dragging a second trebuchet out of the wreckage and loading it with a flint boulder.

The airship zoomed past again, except this time before the hamsta blew apart more of the resistance forces, the boulder came flying and smashed the prow of the ship to pieces. Pieces of wooden debris as well as Velostic's soldiers were thrown into the air before they, and the remains of the ship, came crashing down onto the bloody melee that had broken out on the ground.

Through the choking dust cloud that hung over the wreckage and the confusion of the battlefield, the Templarians could make out a line of dark shapes. Dark shapes advancing... The enemy forces had regrouped and were charging at them at an alarming speed.

"You will not sssssssurvive," hissed one of the basilisks, as their slithering ranks rose up to defend the Templarians.

His voice was fazed out by the screaming of Velostic's heartless army. They could see a few of Velostic's soldiers emerging from the mammoth–like dust cloud, armed to the teeth with swords and arrows. The basilisks stopped for a moment and gathered into a tight huddle... After 10 seconds they whipped out their freshly sharpened poison tipped spears. The leader, however, brandished a threatening mace. The Templarians looked on in amazement – it was Arda! He looked far more fearsome than he had seemed capable of when they knew him before as the head of food processing...

At this moment, a pack of wolf–life creatures descended onto the plain, it was the Lykonian Regiment, led by Ikari. The leader was happy to have led his kin from the jungle to aid his mistress, at any cost. The lykos bared their fangs and sharpened their claws.

"Charge!" yelled Arda, taking charge of his basilisks. Ikari snarled incomprehensible commands to the legions of lykos as they galloped headlong into the fight. Snakes and soldiers crashed towards each other, becoming indistinguishable in the clamour of shouts, clashing spears and biting basilisk fangs. Lyko tore ruthlessly into leopardi, wolves viciously fighting cats, howls and whimpers filling the air. Both teams showed no sympathy toward each other.

Suddenly Velostic appeared from the dust cloud with a double sided spear. He looked menacing as he approached wielding his unusual weapon, especially as he faded in and out of a shadowy veil. Horrified, onlookers were reminded of his status as a shade.

"Oh no!" cried the basilisk leader, in a panic.

Many soldiers from all sides fell to the ground. There was no consideration for what they have done in their lives. They could have been the second coming of Saint Nicholas! Death does not favour the bold, nor did they favour anyone else. There was no cheating death. In the chaos, the forces of the crumbling Templar stronghold could not escape. After all they would go through, the death toll would be of insurmountable levels.

Thousands were dead, fallen in every corner, wherever you went. Yet to those governing the front lines, death was just another cost to their ambition.

Rorwa had sneaked off to gather resources and make her way through a side-street, through the fortifications. She could only hear screams of rage. The basilisk's strategy was a simple one: charge! On the other side, the Templarians used their significantly smaller army of 20 legionarians (their commanders), commanding legions from 300 to 700 people. The total army size was estimated to be 10,000 strong. The basilisks on the other hand, utilised their stronger bodies and larger army, 100,000 snakes strong. With the added force of the lykos, they were almost unbeatable.

Rorwa looked behind her, and to her surprise, there was a guard. Their sword swung towards her, she was defenceless, but not without her wits. She kicked the knee of the soldier, sending him reeling. She had enough time to find the jackpot, at the time. A sort of javelin, with the ability to extend to a long pole, according to the label which it wore, proud in the forefront of the weapon shop. She knew what to do.

She broke through the window of the store, grabbing the newly found weapon, ripping off the label, of course. The guard was catching up, and in a flurry of seconds, Rorwa swung at the head of the guard, and it connected.

The guard fell to the ground, his body faltering in and out of consciousness as he crumbled to the ground.

"Tell my brothe–" he breathed heavily, "Tha–"

No more. Nothing. There was no cheating the Reaper. A life was gone from the world. Her actions were the cause of someone's last moment. It wasn't her fault, was it though?

But she was the one who delivered that last blow – right?

The fighting had reached its peak now. Someone shot an arrow and killed another basilisk, but the fighting raged on. Both sides were having heavy casualties. Mark and Nooble used their shields to barge like bulls into the soldiers and bash their heads. Mark was suddenly on the danger end of a very sharp spear. It grazed Mark on the arm. He winced and clutched his elbow. The soldier then charged at Nooble and the spear turned suddenly and sent Mark flying through the air. Then, he landed in the front and middle of the basilisks, and next to the leader.

Mark looked up and dodged the swords, knife, bow and arrows and boots of the soldiers. Then he saw him. Arda – the basilisk who helped the trio escape the basilisk region.

"Arda!" cried Mark happily. Arda had just stabbed another soldier.

"Mark?" asked Arda, shocked to see him so close to him at this point in time.

"LOOK OUT!" cried Mark as a soldier charged at Arda with a murderous look in his eyes. Mark grabbed a spear and swept him off his feet. The soldier crashed onto the ground. "There's no time!" cried Arda, "Who's going to get Velostic?"

"I think Vagar is. Hopefully," said Mark, very worried. He was still looking at Arda in confusion until the snake leader found a moment to explain himself,

"I got Rorwa's letter that she sent by raven! I've been the basilisk Emperor ever since my counter–coup against the nobility was successful, and since I owe much of that success to you Templarians, I thought I should come and help!" There wasn't much time for Mark to process all of this, as the pair had to continue fighting off Velostic's loyal soldiers and leopardi.

The relentless basilisks kept on pressing Velostic's army until they started to win, cutting through Velostic's forces like the proverbial hot knife through butter. Some soldiers, tired of fighting, started to faint and surrender, but everyone else still decided to chop the serpentine attackers into dead meat. The basilisks, not taking this kindly, squashed the soldiers flat. In some places, the basilisks and soldiers that had lost their weapons started wrestling each other to the ground. It just became chaos, more than a battle. Someone took a pole and smashed over a couple of basilisks' heads. Then Arda yelled:

"FINISH THEM, AND FORCE THEM TO SURRENDER! Any soldier who does not lay down their weapons will be eaten!" The basilisks had reinforcements, so they battered down the wall of soldiers and kindly asked them to surrender. The soldiers started deserting and ran into the city.

"VICTORY!" yelled Arda, triumphantly, and toppled a guard's lookout post to the ground.

Velostic's aide rushed around in a panic because the Basilisks, aided by the lykos, had somehow made their way through the 'foolproof' defences.

"How is this possible!?" exclaimed one of Velostic's soldiers, "We worked so hard on the defences but clearly they aren't good enough!"

The Grandmaster's troops couldn't figure out how they did it.

"Haha!" yelled one of the basilisks, "Theres no sssstopping us now!" This concerned Velostic's men even more. Because not only were the basilisks Velostic's idea of 'defences', but they were also crazily dangerous.

"That's not our only problem," whispered one of the men who was now very worried.

"What is it ?" asked another one.

"Well..."

"Spit it out then we've not got all day!"

"VELOSTIC IS DEAD!" screamed the worried man. Rumours were spreading through the chaos. Now they had a new problem on their hands but they had to focus on the battle. They tried their best to ignore it and battle on, but with that on their minds, they could not fight to their best abilities. If they surrendered, they might have had a chance but that was a risk that they weren't sure they wanted to take...

"Should we do it?" asked one of the soldiers.

"Uhhhhhhhh... AHHHHHHHHHHH!" screamed the other one. They didn't have time to think because without their leader, they were fighting a losing battle...

As doubts spread through his men, Velostic himself was preparing his escape by sky–shuttle. He sensed the approach of defeat, desertion, or worst of all, mutiny. Perhaps some part of him felt a shred of relief at abandoning the position Clover had chosen for him.

Time waned, each passing moment dwindling for Rorwa, the valiant Templar knight. She sensed Velostic would try to escape while he still could. High above, the shuttle sailed through the expanse, carrying Velostic's hopes. Rorwa, resolute, drew her bow and held her breath. Her aim was true and the fire arrow hit home, engulfing the shuttle in flames.

In moments her satisfaction turned to horror. The vessel hurtled down towards the Templar heroes – Nooble, his brother, James and Arcus. Debris scattered as they sought shelter amid the turmoil. As smoke rose from the twisted wreckage, Rorwa stared in stunned disbelief. Where were her comrades? Would they rise Lazarus–like from the dust – battered yet undeterred?

None would rise – only Velostic emerged from the smouldering ruins, his escape plans now as twisted as the fallen shuttle. With it his heart grew colder. Seeing the glinting of Rorwa's bow across the plain, he vowed to destroy the remaining Templarians that had stood so steadfastly in his way.

Chapter 19

Out of the Ashes

Velostic, fleeing from the crash site, was followed in hot pursuit by Vagar and Yshkavis. They stalked him through the wreckage of toppled battlements and ruined buildings, following the dark aura he omitted. Clutching their weapons tightly, the two advanced into a dark, stony chamber, where the cloaked figure of Velostic was standing. He seemed relaxed. As he stood eyeing his pillaged city through a narrow window, there was an air of indifference about him.

"Cousin, I knew you were going to come, ever since I beat you all those years ago," said Velostic as he turned around. Vagar's eyes nearly popped out of his head – the once proud and strict face of his old companion was turned into one of pain. His eyes that were once a bright, almost electric purple, were now a beaten down purple. His once kind aura of magic was now cold and hollow. Yet the power was still there. His skin was dull, his bone structure was more pronounced. His hands glowed a sickly purple and black. Death Magic.

Then, all of a sudden, Vagar was thrown back against the wall. His throat felt like it was being crushed. The clothes around him seemed to disappear, leaving him to stand cloakless. His armoured chest, covered in chain mail, deflected the ten ton stone that had been thrown at him.

Finally, he broke the ghost's magical grip. Lifting up his axe, he snarled and swung. A bewildered Velostic was sent flying, the blow stripping him of his magical armour as it disintegrated.

Vagar lifted the weapon and swung downwards releasing the handle. The weapon was met by a blast of magic, holding it in place. Velostic reemerged, his hand coated in a sinister purple fire.

"For goodness sake Velostic, who do you think you are? Hecate!" grunted Yshkavis who herself gripped a long spear.

"Well maybe I am," he grunted as he lifted his hands and

swung downwards sending many rocks in his adoring cousin's direction. Vagar seemed to feel the world slow down. His muscles felt frozen. Velostic laughed as he darted forward, his fist rushed downwards onto the shaft of his silver spear, releasing a massive explosion, blasting the prison manager backwards.

Yshkavis growled as she skidded on her knees, skinning them – blood started pouring. She growled a quick healing spell to kill the pain. Then she leapt up, and with the grace of an assassin, launched her spear forward with ease, her anger fueling her attack. Her effort was thwarted by Velostic's undead powers, as he slipped into a portal with a grin spreading across his face. As Yshkavis's spear missed its target, Velostic reappeared out of the ether, his arm raised in attack.

"Duck!" shouted Vagar as he leapt forward, diving to protect Yshkavis. Yshkavis cursed as she tried to drop to dodge the thrust. All of a sudden, she heard a gasp of pain as she hit the ground. Her head whipped around. A sudden feeling of illness hit her. She looked up to see Vagar's stomach had been impaled by Velostic's spear. Velostic stood over him, thinking his work was done. Yshkavis, sensing her enemy's distraction, thrust forward her weapon skewering Velostic.

Velostic bolted backwards, gripping his wound. He growled a powerful healing spell but the wound refused to heal. The magical axe was already inhibiting his powers. She stood up and turned her attention to the dying Vagar. But then she was blasted straight into a wall, her spear flung far away. She tried to stand up and coughed up some blood. Her once cold, pride filled face was covered in blood and grime. She could feel her life–force leaving her body and for the first time ever. She knew she was going to die.

Suddenly, an invisible hand gripped her by her throat, lifting her off the floor. Velostic was spending the very last of his magic ensuring her demise. She closed her eyes and she felt the breath leave her body for the last time.

Velostic growled as he dragged himself across the floor. He was dying and he knew it was probably deserved after murdering his cousin. Once again, he looked down on the battlefield.

"Well I see you have lost," said a voice beside him.

"Yes, I guess I did," he said as he looked out on the bloodstained ground. The cloaked speaker sat down next to him.

"I wish it didn't have to be this way," he said as he crushed a piece of rock easily.

"Well whoever you are, thank you for occupying me in my final moments," Velostic said almost silently, as his soul ebbed away.

"All is well," said the person as he turned to look at him. His hair was white and a pair of red eyes broke up the blackness of his shadowy face.

The battle was ending, and the Basilisks started slithering through the city walls. The guards surrendered and hid behind some crates. The Basilisk Flag was raised over the strategic buildings of the city. No civilians had been killed, but there were casualties – wounded people and dead soldiers. Then finally, they overran the Templarian Headquarters. Everyone was taken by surprise, and retreated out through the back door. The alarm sounded and was broken by a basilisk, and then they stormed the place and took over the control room, followed by the main Templarian chamber. Suddenly, Arda halted them. In front of them, there was the face of the Vice–Grandmaster.

"Please..." he begged. "I surrender. I had nothing to do with this! I was only following orders, I once had the thought of killing him, but that was too hard, and that was a few days before the storming of Templarian City." Arda stopped and beckoned him to get up.

"Ok, you're spared," he said. "But your country is surrendering and you must announce to the city that Velostic is dead." The Vice–Grandmaster left the room quickly.

A few minutes later, it was announced that the Vice–Grandmaster had surrendered to the Basilisks and Velostic was dead. The Basilisks cheered, and all around the city, everyone celebrated, except for a section of hardcore Velostic supporters. They started moaning and protesting that they didn't have anything against the basilisks.

Chapter 20

One Last Sacrifice

Clover was in front of them, holding the cold cloak of what used to be Velostic.

"Well, look who finally showed their face," Rorwa sighed.

Clover laughed. "How cynical of you to assume that I'm only here for the kill."

"So you aren't?" Mark charged up his magic.

"Nay, lad." He replied, "People aren't 2D, unlike in a story."

Rorwa looked at him, confused. "Eh?"

Mark launched his magic spell, "Ecauridian!" It was his signature move, the one shot punch of spells. This was sure to get the kill on this villain, right?

Wrong. "I'm not weak enough to be beaten by a spell," Clover boomed.

The spell bounced off his cloak, ricocheting around before landing in Clover's hand.

Rorwa charged towards Clover, using many magic spells to create a flurry of blasts and strikes. Mark joined in with this rush of spells. But they had no effect.

Clover saw that Rorwa seemingly disappeared, only to bring down the walls.

The entire basilisk army was advancing behind her. Clover stared on in shock, as he thought he, Rorwa, and Mark were the only ones there.

The basilisks poured in from all sides, one by one charging towards Clover. This looked like the end for Clover. Except, the basilisks had an ancient problem, the reptilian aversion for the cold. That was why they resided in the crystal caverns beneath the warmth of the desert. And Clover had access to a type of magic, ice magic to be exact. A snow storm swept through the small area the fight was contained in, and the basilisks started slithering out in waves. The cavalry was gone. Hope was gone.

"You're a monster!" Rorwa screamed.

"Don't think you're any better." Clover retorted, "My mum didn't deserve to die, Alessandro didn't deserve to die." He screamed.

Yet there still was a plan.

Mark lined up in front of Clover, the man who had ended the lives of so many. Mark's mind raced, full of questions about the man's motives. Was he driven by the inhumane pleasure of watching others suffer? Or was this psychopathy? Mark couldn't understand what had driven his maniacal plan.

There was a reason. But that was not important, not anymore. At least to the Templars. But to Clover it was everything.

Think back to the start and see the hidden messages stuck in plain sight, in a new light. He had been seeking revenge all along.

Mark fought one to one with the deadliest mage on the planet, barely holding on. Clover drew on the dark magic he had become a master of; Mark conjured the power of the runes he had spent years studying. The weight of the fight pulled him down. How would he win? The two were bound together in the frenzy of spells. A realisation crept over Mark. The thing is, he didn't have to win, or even survive. He just needed to stall.

This was the nature of the 'plan'. Everyone watching, especially Rorwa, began to understand that Mark was willing to sacrifice himself. The old companions had an almost telekinetic understanding that didn't need a spoken agreement. Rorwa knew what she had to do.

"Well. This is the end. For both of us." Mark laughed. "If only it wasn't so bloody."

"Smart move," Clover said, knowing he couldn't relinquish his spell on Mark or he alone would perish.

Rorwa had climbed to the top of the tower nearby, it was one of the few castle defences still standing. The lever was in front of her. If she pulled it, the ballista would fire and Clover would die. But Mark, she thought. She hesitated.

The lever flicked.

"I've done enough," said Clover, "Maybe we'll be friends in another life."

Then, the ballista's missile homed in on Mark and Clover, who were eternally locked in a magical death–duel. And then there was nothing.

The end.

Our story is done. Almost…

Those who perished that day, caught between the forces of Clover's desire for revenge and the Templarian's quest to restore justice, would never get the chance to tell their story. Nooble, who had come so far from being an unlucky knight-in-training, was one such casualty. He died clutching his luckier brother Blooble in false hope of survival, as Velostic's sinking airship torpedoed towards them. Now they lay together in the rubble alongside two other friends.

Rorwa alone could reflect on the Templarians' victory, made bittersweet by the knowledge of her comrades' sacrifices. After all, history is written by the winners, or the survivor, in this case.

Epilogue

Rorwa looked out over the battlefield, you could barely see the rugged earth for blood and bodies. She could find no reason to justify so many deaths, an amount she couldn't comprehend. Often the superiors higher up found it easy to send men to their deaths, and common people paid the price for such hollow victories. Her eyes found the body of her comrade Vagar. She eased the spear from his hand and found that even in death his fingers were still clenched tight with a warrior's grip. She picked up the spear, a symbol of suffering, and cast it aside where it embedded itself into the body of one of the senators who had appeared at the battle to raise the morale. Rorwa sighed deeply, forcing away thoughts of a future that could have been. She would mourn Vagar later, for now she had to find out the fate of her other friends.

Another part of her life had been lost, just like her mother and father had been long before.

Epilogue Part 2. 1 Year Later

Rorwa walked outside of her new house. The day was stormy. She sat down on the bench nearby, but something caught her attention. A man with red eyes and spiky hair, in a midnight black gown. Though she had never seen him before, there was a familiar glint in his eye as he looked up at Rorwa.

The man smiled, yet Rorwa sensed something deeply threatening about him. With almost cinematic timing, the sky flashed and a bolt of lightning cracked in the distance. Rorwa turned to assess the darkening storm clouds, as thunder bellowed over the city. By the time she turned back to the mysterious stranger, he was gone.